Loving Arms
Can Haunt You

Historical Books by Dianna Cross Toran

Woodland Echoes – A Cottage in My Heart
Shadows Beyond the Pines

LOVING ARMS
CAN HAUNT YOU

To Marla,
My Woodland
Park neighbor and
friend. Love the 'Little
Cottage'!
Best Regards
Dianna
Cross
Toran

Dianna Cross Toran

Library of Congress Control Number:		2022911598
ISBN:	Hardcover	978-1-6698-3467-0
	Softcover	978-1-6698-3466-3
	eBook	978-1-6698-3465-6

Rev. date: 06/21/2022

To order additional copies of this book, contact:
Xlibris
844-714-8691
www.Xlibris.com
Orders@Xlibris.com
842878

For my family and friends

ACKNOWLEDGMENTS

Writing a murder mystery is different from writing about history. I wasn't so sure I was on target with this book until I asked my sister-in-law, Marion Polk, to read my manuscript. With her encouragement, I decided to step outside the box and publish *Loving Arms Can Haunt You*. Special thanks to Marian Polk. I would also like to give special thanks to my niece, Desiree Polk-Bland for my cover photograph.

CHAPTER 1

My name is Willamina Rivers. I got the Willamina name from some long-passed relative that now I'm stuck with it, but everyone calls me Billie. I am petite, a pretty word for short; have dark curly brown hair (kind of like Halle Berry's in the movie *The Call* but longer) that has a mind of its own; and a light brown complexion that was given to me by the mixture of black, white, and Cherokee blood on both sides of the family. Momma often said, "Your people were shackled in the bottom of the ship, running things topside and meeting it when it first arrived in America. Umm hum." She would always end these kinds of talks with an "Umm hum" with her lips pursed and her eyebrows raised.

Momma is short like me, dark brown in color, has hair the color of honey (dyed of course), and very pretty. She loves listening to the Motown sound and passed that love on to her children, me and Georgie. There is no rap played in her house, period. She is on the thin side and because she was so short you wouldn't think she could sometimes be a bit scary. But she is. My momma didn't play. She was the executioner in our family, and her choice of weapon was an Avon brush.

Pops is tall, light in color, and had straight jet-black hair with sprinkles of gray. He is cool and is always the voice of reason until he is behind the wheel of a car. Then periodically he sounds like he has Tourette syndrome and shouts out about something dumb someone just did in another vehicle even though he sometimes does the same things himself. He and Momma are both teachers. That meant Georgie and I (notice how I said that properly) are always in a classroom, especially at home.

My sister's name is really Georgia, but we call her Georgie. Pops clearly wanted boys. Georgie has the same complexion and curly hair that I have.

1

She is a bit on the bossy side and can't keep a secret if her life depended on it. As children, we kept our parents on their toes. We both hated to see Momma carrying an Avon bag. As adults, we would still have our disagreements from time to time, but Georgie would always come to my aid if I needed her, and I had her back if she needed me.

For as long as I can remember, my family spent a lot of time at our family place in the Enchanted Woods Village in Michigan. For the month of July, we would run the family business, the Loving Arms Inn, while my Aunt Mae and Uncle James would take a much-needed vacation. Aunt Mae and Uncle James were Pop's aunt and uncle. Both Pop's and Momma's parents died long before I was born, so our aunt and uncle had been like parents to Pops and Momma and grandparents to me and Georgie.

The roads that led back to the Village were all dusty dirt roads that had been cut through sand decades ago. The roads had multiple ruts that never seemed to be filled in that made us bounce around in our old Pontiac Bonneville. We would stand up in the backseat and hang on to the front seat (we didn't use seatbelts back then, and I don't recall there being any in the car), almost bumping our heads on the ceiling of the car as we maneuvered through holes. Pops would hit almost all of them and would mutter a cuss word with every bounce, making Georgie and me giggle. Momma would "Tsk" and say, "Harvey Jameson Rivers, you better watch your mouth. You have little ears that hear everything and repeat it. Umm hum."

"But Anita, did you just see what they just did?" Then a fresh set of cuss words would be muttered that would make us giggle.

Looking out the car windows, through all the dust we would kick up along the way we would see cattails, berries of all kinds and wildflowers that grew along the roadside. The excitement inside the car would build as we pulled into town. We loved our little tourist resort and all the shops and businesses in the main part of the village. We knew everyone, and we were known by everyone. People of all colors happily walked around or shopped, ate, or drank at all the local businesses. Everyone waved as we passed, and we waved in return.

The "Village," as we all called it, was way off the main roads and deep in the forest. The town was built around a beautiful spring-fed lake that has many water-lilied coves and shallows. It had great fishing too, and even though the fish outsmart most, there were many impressive catches that kept the fishermen interested. The sandy shoreline was perfect for young swimmers, and the deeper waters were great for the many boats and jet skis. It was calm enough in the no-wake areas for the kayakers and paddle boards. At one time the Village had been a successful black resort during segregation and, before then, an old lumber mill. It was so off the beaten path that I often thought that Lewis and Clark would have had trouble finding it. It is beautiful and perfect.

We would drive around the contour of the lake until we would get to our turnoff on a short two-track driveway. A hand-carved wooden sign always greeted us that said, "Welcome All to the Loving Arms Inn." The Inn itself didn't sit very far from the road, and the lake could be seen behind it. The Inn was a well-kept, beautiful, old-fashioned two-story structure with an attic, built out of logs that were cut from the area when the old Bradford Saw Mill had been there. From what people knew about its history, the Inn had once been the home of Jackson Bradford, the owner of the mill, built in 1853 for his family. But the winters were so harsh that he couldn't sell his wife on joining him there with the new baby, so they never lived in it, preferring instead to live in one of their other homes in the warm weather of the Southern states.

The log house had been taken care of by a black caretaker according to folklore that had been passed on through the years. Many years later, when my grandparents, Uncle James, and Aunt Mae bought it, they turned it into a hotel and named it the Loving Arms Inn. When my grandparents passed, they left their half to Pops. Pops went off to college, met Momma, and they decided to make the city their home. They love the Inn, but they weren't interested in it being their full-time jobs. They loved being teachers. Both Pops and Momma were teachers at the same elementary school, the same school both Georgie and I attended. You think it was bad having one parent a teacher there? Well, try having two. Geesh!

Aunt Mae is of average height, a bit heavy in the hips, and hair that was silver and beautiful. She wore it cut short. She was nurturing and sweet. She is very well-read too. She graduated from Wilberforce with a nursing degree but never used it. She owns many books and reads them frequently. She loves to play the piano and tried her best to teach Georgie and me how to play. No chopsticks. Uncle James looks like an older version of Pops. He had been married before, but that was before Georgie and I were born. He loves to listen to jazz and puff away on his cigar. He is a reader too and loves to read murder mysteries. I probably inherited that trait from him because I really love curling up with a cozy murder mystery.

We loved our July vacation although it wasn't a vacation for our parents. As soon as we would arrive, Georgie and I would rush out of the car and run up the wooden steps into the large screened-in porch. Baskets of colorful flowers hung from hooks strategically placed. Georgie and I would race to see who got to the door first and would both pull it open. The old screen door would groan and then slam behind us. Then it was a race for the prize we knew was waiting for us. We would race like we were being chased by Momma and her brush to the office. Our destination was a large wooden desk where we knew there would be a fresh supply of our favorite candy (which would be any kind of candy) left for us by Aunt Mae in a secret compartment in the leg of the desk.

Uncle James and Aunt Mae were a kind couple who never had children of their own. The Loving Arms, Georgie, and I seem to be all the responsibilities they wanted. There would always be some kind of blowup toy, boats, pails, and shovels for us to play with in the water or on the beach when it was sunny. They would have coloring books, crayons, finger paints, and all other kinds of goodies that would keep us occupied on rainy days. Aunt Mae made the best chocolate chip cookies that we would eat when they weren't quite cooled off. We would have chocolate all over our fingers and faces. Uncle James made us a tiny raft that we would sit on and wait for boats to go by so that we could ride the waves in our pink Barbie life jackets. It remained tied to the dock in about two feet of water because we weren't allowed to go out on our own—well, except for one time when we did, and unlucky for us, Momma brought that dreaded Avon brush with her.

Being children, we didn't appreciate how every room inside the Inn had beautiful glistening hardwood floors and lavish wood trim around all the doors and windows. The windows in the main rooms and bedrooms had window seats with cushions and pillows. Beneath each window seat was storage where Georgie and I would often hide some of our toys. Some of the windows were made of brightly colored stained-glass artworks with flowers, birds, butterflies, and wildlife. Aunt Mae made up stories about each of them that she would tell me and Georgie whenever we were in that room. All the doorknobs and such were made from what was once shiny brass that had aged beautifully over many years. The light fixtures were made of intricate brass and glass and reflected the light on the ceilings and walls. In the main hall was a chandelier that greeted guests as they arrived. There were front stairs and back stairs, all made with carved wood. The front stairs were wide and curved around to the lobby, and the back stairs were narrow and led straight to the kitchen. The large kitchen, though updated for modern appliances, still had most of its antique flavor. There was a butler's pantry too. There was a common room just off the main entrance. It was large and had comfortable leather chairs and sofas and a large bar where Uncle James would fix me and Georgie little play cocktails with cherries and umbrellas (nonalcoholic of course).

There were five large rooms for rent on the main floor, the living quarters for my aunt and uncle, six rooms on the second floor, and one great room in the attic room that was more of a suite. Each rental room had shiny numbers hanging on them. Our Inn was old-fashioned, so the doors all had a skeleton key, but usually no one locked them unless they were city folk. Most of the rooms had their own bathrooms with claw-foot tubs and stained-glass windows of hummingbirds or flowers. It had a creepy old basement that Georgie and I never went in. That was where Aunt Mae did the laundry and stored a lot of old furniture that was no longer being used. The attic room was my favorite and the one my family always stayed in. It was large enough to play in and had a large window in the front with a view of the road and one in the back with a view of the lake.

Next door was the Water's Edge Tavern. It was another family-owned business passed down from a generation or two. It was owned by the McGuires. John and Tony McGuire had been like brothers to me and Georgie. Our family was theirs, and their family was ours. Momma took a brush to both John and Tony a few times, and Mrs. McGuire, or Aunt Birdie as we called her, had licked me and Georgie a few times as well. Uncle Pete (Mr. McGuire) built me and Georgie a beautiful dollhouse that Georgie's girls now play with.

CHAPTER 2

For as long as I live, I will remember one summer at the Inn when I was six. As usual, we children filled our days playing with all the local kids, biking, fishing, and picking blueberries and raspberries that grew along our fence. We had the best beach on the lake, so everyone would come and swim there. It was always crowded. I remember after a full morning on our beach, John, Tony, Georgie, and I ran across the road to the corner store, the Bait Shop. At the door, we all stopped and pulled out our pockets. I was a smart six-year-old. I never carried my money in my pockets.

"Who has money?" John, Tony, and Georgie would all say in unison or almost unison. They all looked at what they just pulled out of their pockets. A lot of stones, shells, dried worms, and some change. I didn't pull out mine because I knew nothing would be in them. Then they all looked at me.

"Billie. You have money in one of your socks. Momma gave it to you this morning, and I saw you put it there." Never have your sister be an eyewitness to anything you want kept secret.

I blew air through my clenched lips like I always do when experiencing stress.

"But I was saving my money for a super soaker," I whined.

"Come on, Billie. Momma said you couldn't have one anyway." Then it became the "she did not–did to" debate, eventually ending with me giving up my two dollars. We went inside and carefully picked out our candy and put it up on the counter. Mrs. Josephine Baits, who ran the Bait Shop grocery store, took our money and gave us each our own little bags so that we could divvy up what we bought. She was used to having a lot of little kids in her store, especially us. Mrs. Baits had been a teacher when the one-room schoolhouse was in operation during segregation. Then she went to work for the public school when the schools were integrated. When she retired, she took over her father's grocery store, the Bait Shop. She was tall, heavy, and brown in color. She wore glasses that she would peer over when she spoke to you. If you wanted to know what was going on in our little village, all you had to do was make a trip over to the Bait Shop. She had all the news.

"I see Pete bought a new truck," she said, peering over her glasses at John.

"Yes, ma'am." John kind of rocked from side to side. He wanted to get to his candy. We all did, but you couldn't speed up or walk away from Mrs. Baits. She was going to grill you for information.

"Did he get it in Grand Rapids?"

"No, ma'am. He got it in Detroit."

"Oh, he probably special-ordered it. You don't know how much he paid for it, do you?" She was hoping that John or Tony overheard their father talking about it.

"No, ma'am." She may have interrogated the enemy during the war because this line of questioning went on for a while until someone else came into the store. We were glad to hear the tinkle of the little bell over the door, indicating a new customer had entered and that we were free to go. We quickly made our escape out the door and sat on the grass beside the store. We divvied up our purchases and then went about eating our candy. Someone must have dropped a dollar in their haste to get away from Mrs. Baits because Georgie found it lying in the grass, and she and John went back in the store for more candy and interrogation. Me and Tony were sitting on the grass waiting. I was happily chewing away on my Airhead. Tony reached into his bag and gave me an extra piece of his candy for letting us have my two dollars.

"Here, Billie. But don't tell John or Georgie that I gave it to you." He handed me a Kit Kat. He looked around, and finding no one else in earshot, he said, "Someday I'm going to marry you." Then he kissed me on my cheek.

I was horrified and said, "Ewwww. Oh no you're not." With that, I got up and ran into the store. Tony ran after me to make sure I didn't tell.

Later that day Georgie and I were playing skating rink in the attic. We had taken off our shoes, and with a running start, we slid across the floor to see who could slide the longest. We squealed with laughter. When we got tired of "skating," we decided to snoop. The Inn had all kinds of little nooks and crannies. Except for the basement, which we never went down there because it was creepy, we often explored every room unless there was a guest in it. Up in the attic room, there was one mysterious door that instead of a number hanging on it, there was a sign on it that said "Private – Keep Out." It didn't keep me and Georgie from trying the door every time we visited, but it was always locked. Eventually Georgie and I gave the door the name "Private." On that same day, Georgie had just given Private a good tug. It still didn't budge. We stood there looking at it in our socks.

"What do you think's in Private, Georgie?" I asked.

"Uncle James said it's a room with monsters, witches, and ghosts. That's why they have to lock it," said Georgie. Being the oldest by almost two years, she felt like she had to scare me from time to time. I guess my face told her that she hit her target and she ran out the door and down the steps laughing all the way. Scared that she may be right, I ran off behind her.

"Aaaaaaaaah!" I screamed my head off. But because of my slippery socks, I didn't quite make it through the door and ran right into it. I hit my head, fell flat on my back, and saw flashes of light. I almost fainted. While lying on the floor, I heard a creaking noise coming from the direction of Private. I slowly turned my head, bringing it into view. I saw that Private was now open, and an old black man in old-fashioned clothes was peeking out of it, looking at me. Still laying on the floor, I started screaming again—"Aaaaaaaaah!"—and I could have sworn he did too before he disappeared into thin air. Then I did faint.

CHAPTER 3

We still came up in July to the Loving Arms Inn every year after that weird time. Everyone chalked it up to a little girl's wild imagination, and I stayed away from Private as much as possible in case it wasn't. Eventually I put the old man in the back of my mind and figured everyone must be right; I must have made him up. When I graduated high school and was thinking about college and a career, I found a job up the street from where I lived at the local hotel. I guess I was hooked on the hotel business from my summers at the Loving Arms. I cleaned rooms with a lot of nice ladies who pretended not to be able to speak English to the guest, but they spoke excellent English to me.

One day, I asked Rosita, one of the more talkative ladies, why they pretended not to speak English, and she told me in perfect English, "You would be surprised at what people ask you to do because they think we are some dumb immigrants who wouldn't know any better. So, we pretend we don't understand. I was born here. I am just short of my master's in electrical engineering. And the beauty of this is we can talk about them to each other, and they don't know what we are saying." Then she said something in rapid Spanish to the other ladies that I couldn't quite make out with my limited high school Spanish, and they all looked at me and had a good laugh. "See what I mean?" she said.

I ended up going to Ferris State to get my degree in hospitality. I worked my way up in the neighborhood hotel for years, and by the time I got my degree, I was working for Embassy Suites in Customer Services. I was there for some time and was really good at my job. Since I still lived at home, I was able to sock away a nice nest egg as Momma called it. I had a handsome fiancé, Michael Morris, who I now call Pig Slop, who also worked at the Embassy Suites. When Pig Slop asked me to marry him, I thought we were going to have a beautiful wedding, buy a nice home, and move up in the hotel business together. I was Ms. Living-in-a-World-of-Make-Believe and would happily tell my coworkers about our wedding plans.

On my thirtieth birthday, some of my coworkers threw me a little party at our Embassy Suites bar. For days, I noticed one of them from HR kept looking like she wanted to tell me something. After I had some Jack Daniel's and she a few Crown Royals, she gave me a copy of Pig Slop's personnel file that she smuggled out of the office. According to his 1099, he already had a wife and two kids. I got right up off of that bar stool and almost did a face plant. Luckily, I was caught by some guy who happened to be walking by. I straightened myself out and walked over to the center of the atrium where Pig Slop was talking to a guest. Under the circumstances you would have thought I would have made a scene. Ha ha! You bet your sweet bippy I did. Right in the atrium where everyone could see on every floor, all eight. "You, you, you, *Pig Slop!*" I was so mad I didn't know what I was saying or doing. I picked up anything I could lay my hands on and threw it at him. It was well worth the night I spent in jail.

Pops picked me up after Momma paid the bail. I climbed into the backseat and stared out the window. On the way home, I was waiting for the lecture. Instead, Momma said, "Billie, I know things seem a bit difficult right now, but this will pass. You have all your future ahead of you and a loving family behind you." She talked for a while about how I would look back at this one day and laugh. "It will start out as a smile . . ." she droned on. It started to sound like blah, blah, blah to me as she kept talking.

Pops had been silent up until then. I guess waiting for his chance to say something that never came, so he butted in. "Anita, will you let me say something?" Momma sucked in a deep breath and just stared at him. *Here it comes*, I thought. "Billie, I want you to know that while your momma was working on bailing you out, I went over to the hotel and punched Michael in the nose. I felt it break." I saw Momma smile at him. Without another word, we continued home. I smiled. I love my Pops.

For about a week, I stayed in my room and sulked. Georgie, who was married and had a couple of the cutest girls that anyone could have, would come over and try to get me out of my dungeon.

"Billie, you can't keep this up." She of all people should know that isn't true. I've sulked before. Besides, I had no rent to pay, I still had multiple episodes of the *Fresh Prince of Bel-Air* to binge-watch, and Grub Hub still accepted my credit card. "You are acting like you did something wrong, but you didn't. *He did*." I think you should also know that she is talking to the outside of my bedroom door because I wouldn't let her in, or about now, I would be slamming the door in her face. Why, if I wasn't in bed with the shades pulled; my hair all over my head; terrible week-old morning, noon, and night breath; and the same PJs that I put on when I got home after my night in the big house, I would really let that door swing shut in her face.

"Stop acting like a big baby. This isn't all that bad." Oh no? I've been fired, humiliated, and arrested. I have a court appearance coming up and may have to do some time in the big house. I don't know because I've never been arrested before. She obviously hasn't researched all the facts and needs to work on her pep talk. "You just need to suck it up!" Oh no she didn't! She finally gave up and left in disgust. I stuck my tongue out in the direction of the door.

I had lots of friends who tried to cheer me up. At first I answered calls, but when my friends started asking me about what happened, I acted like there was something wrong with my phone and hung up. I would look at my texts now and then until one of my friends sent me a YouTube link to, you guessed it, me and Pig Slop arguing in the atrium. Actually, he was mostly cowering while I yelled at him and threw whatever was nearby. I watched myself in horror as I yelled, "You, you, you, *Pig Slop!*" It racked up a lot of hits. At that point, I stopped taking calls or looking at Facebook completely. I didn't turn off my cell, and I still looked to see who was calling, but I didn't pick up until one call caught my attention. It was from the Embassy Suites, so I picked it up. I had hoped it was Pig Slop so that I could say a few more choice words to him, but it wasn't.

"Hi, Willamina." Only supervisors from the Embassy Suites and my teachers called me that. "This is Jessica Jamison-Smith. I believe we have met a few times." That made me sit upright. She was my ex-supervisor's boss. Uh-oh! Now what?

"Ah, hi. I am really sorry for my behavior. I have never done anything like that before and will never do it again." I wasn't sorry, but I was sure that is what she wanted to hear. Hello, orange jumpsuits. Truth be told and I had it all to do over, I would do it again.

"Don't apologize. I found out the whole story, and although I can't hire you back, I have made sure that the charges were dropped." My mouth dropped open.

"Thank you. I don't know what to say."

"You aren't the only one this has happened to." Seems she may have been a victim of love sometime before or after the hyphen in her name. She lowered her voice some and said, "Just between you and me I think he is ——." Yikes, does that woman have a sailor's mouth. "I also gave Mr. Morris his walking papers, if it helps." Yes, it does!

"Thank you" was all I could think to say. We hung up. I smiled. I no longer had to worry about if I needed to buy a tin cup and learn the words to "Nobody Knows the Trouble I've Seen." But I still wasn't motivated to get up. I grabbed the edge of my blanket and threw myself under it as I fell back into my bed.

CHAPTER 4

I heard a soft knock at my door. Actually, it was a loud banging. I blew air through my clenched lips.

"Billie, it's Momma. You need to get back to living. I gave you a week to get it together, but the week is up." She waited for a nanosecond before she gave me an ultimatum. Then she banged on the door with every word. "Don't. Make. Me. Come. In. There. Either you open the door, or I cut off your cable and food deliveries. I don't know who you think you are that you don't have to leave your room." I sat up. As I said before, I still had some Fresh Prince episodes that I hadn't rewatched yet and didn't want the cable turned off.

"That room is part of *my house*. Do you hear me? *My house*. And another thing. Take a shower and brush your teeth. You stink. Umm hum."

"Oh, before I forget, a letter came for you." She slid it under my door. "Now get going. Don't make me come back up here and take the door off the hinges. I still have an old Avon brush and haven't forgotten how to use it." That wasn't an idle threat about the door. The last time she had Pops take off the door, it was a month before she let Pops put it back up. I wasn't too sure if the Avon brush was an idle threat either. It's been a while. I heard her muttering under her breath as she stomped away.

Besides, she had piqued my curiosity. Who writes letters in this century? You text, e-mail, Zoom, or communicate many other ways, but nobody writes a letter. I got up and stubbed my big toe on the nightstand because it was so dark in the room. Limping, I felt my way to the door, and before picking up the letter, I turned on the light. I reached down and pulled it out from under the door. The return address showed it was from

---

Aunt Mae. I should have known. I tore it open. It was short and to the point, just like Aunt Mae. Her penmanship was stellar too.

Dear Billie,

Your Uncle and I were wondering if you would come and spend the spring and summer helping us out at the Inn. I know you have your life and your job there in the city, but it would really be helpful to us if you would please give us a hand. We are getting a bit old and not running the place as well as we would like.

Please come as soon as possible.

Sincerely,
Aunt Mae

Now I'm not gullible. I'm pretty sure my parents had something to do with this, but I didn't have any other options that would enable me to sulk and keep my bedroom door. I took Momma's advice and showered and brushed my teeth, put on fresh clothes, and threw the PJs I had been wearing all week in the trash. As I was packing my bag, Momma came into my room, took a sniff, and immediately went to the window and opened it up.

"Glad you decided to join the living."

"Um, sorry, Momma, for being such a pain."

"You aren't a pain, Billie. Well, maybe a small one sometimes, but you have a good head on your shoulders."

"Guess what? The charges have been dropped. Aunt Mae wrote that letter. She wants me to come for the spring and summer." I didn't tell her about Pig Slop being fired. "Did you call Uncle James and Aunt Mae?"

I saw her hesitate for a moment before she said, "Does it really matter? You have always loved the Village and that old Inn. It always made you happy. You need some of that happy now." Then she looked me deep in the eyes, and her face softened. "You are standing at a crossroad. You can't keep moping in your room without cable, food, and a door. Michael was . . . was . . ." She faltered for a description that was low enough to fit.

I helped her. "Pig Slop?"

"Yes, Pig Slop, and not worth all of this drama. So go take a walk on a new road and leave that one behind." I reached out to her and hugged her like my life depended on it. She hugged me back and whispered in my ear, "I'm so glad you showered and brushed your teeth, or this could have been unbearable." Leave it to Momma.

I finished packing and said my goodbyes to Pops and Momma. They looked relieved. I packed up what would fit in my little red Volkswagen Beetle and headed north to what I thought would be a long unemployed vacation at Loving Arms Inn.

After hours of driving, I pulled into the two-track driveway. My aunt and uncle were standing in front of the Inn waiting for me. The way they stood there so solemn side by side, all that was needed was a pitchfork. They ushered me back to their living quarters, and the way they looked at me, the dam that had temporarily held back my heartbreak once again broke free, and through my tears I unloaded all that I had recently gone through. They were so kind and concerned. Aunt Mae cooed and hugged me as I told them what had happened. Uncle James didn't know what to do, so he quietly listened, clenching and unclenching his hands now and then. I am sure they couldn't make out half of what I told them through all the wailing, but to their credit, they didn't try to stop me and let me just get it out of my system. When I finally ran dry, we all hugged it out, and I really felt better. I was in the place I loved the most, and even though I still harbor thoughts of wanting to pull a Carrie Underwood and dig my key into the side of Pig Slop's car, carve my name into his seats, and take a Louisville slugger to both headlights, I didn't feel quite bad enough to want to slash all four tires. Well, maybe one or two of them but not all four. I thought I was making progress.

CHAPTER 5

Sandy Dixon was lying on her back on her couch, scrolling through her cell phone on Facebook. She would like or comment from time to time. Sandy was a young black woman of questionable values. She was pretty and was one of those girls who had gotten her grown-up curves early in junior high school. She was considered "fast" in school, and the boys knew her well. She wore her hair in long braided extensions, and although she didn't have to, she applied too much makeup every day.

She grew up in the Village in a rundown house that was down one of the dirt roads. It was close to the railroad tracks, and every time a train went through, it was felt in the house. The lot that it sat on was small. Sandy tried to sell it once, but nobody wanted it, so she took it off the market. You had to really want to specifically visit Sandy because there weren't any other homes on that road. Generations of her family had lived in the Village, in that very house, but she was the only one left. She hated the house. She hated the woods. She hated the Village. She was tired of seeing the same old faces every day. What she really wanted was to go to Chicago and live. She dreamed of being somebody. She felt like a nobody here. But she didn't want to venture there without a meal ticket. She had tried it once and ended up right back in that house.

She hated working in that stupid Baits Shop grocery store with that fat, crabby old Mrs. Baits. She thought she could tell Sandy what to do because she had been Sandy's elementary teacher. Sandy resented all the multigenerational businesses. Nobody left Sandy any store or something she could sell to get out of this place. Sandy also hated that tacky little white girl, Sally or Susan or some white-girl name that she couldn't remember. Sally/Susan had just moved into the Village and been working in the store for a few months. She was a hard worker, always helping customers, or if she didn't have anything to do, she would dust or mop the floors. Sandy resented her because she felt she was trying to show her up. Sandy did as little as she could and was often on her cell phone. Old lady Baits would yell at her and tell her to stop being so lazy. If Sandy didn't need the money, she would quit. Being around both old lady Baits and what's-her-name at the store was annoying.

Sandy finally got tired of looking through her phone. She got up, went to her little bedroom, and began looking through her clothes. She started thinking about her secret boyfriend. No one knew about him because when he came to see her, which was often, he made sure no one knew he was coming to see her. He was going to be her ticket out. He could sell his business, and together they could start over again in Chicago. Her mind wandered down that direction for a while. She walked over to her bedroom door and closed it. Attached to it was a full-length mirror. She gazed at her reflection for a long time. She gave herself an approving nod and made up her mind.

"I think I'll just mosey on over to the Water's Edge and see what that cute Tony is doing," she said out loud to no one. She put on a tight low-cut top and a tight pair of jeans. She examined her recent manicure and pedicure. She liked her acrylic nails nice and long and always in brilliant colors. This time they were hot pink. Old lady Baits wanted her to cut them. She said Sandy made too many errors on the register because of them, but Sandy refused. She liked her long nails. She went to the mirror in the bathroom and carefully applied her false eyelashes. It wasn't easy with those nails. She then put on her gold jewelry and tied a colorful bandana around her head. Her long braided extensions flowed down her back.

She grabbed her purse and opened her front door. She jumped in surprise when she saw her secret boyfriend standing there.

"Well, hello, baby. I was just thinking about you. You must have read my mind. Come on in." He didn't say a word; he just picked her up, kicked the door shut, and carried her to the bed.

Rachel Pennington was usually depressed, but today she really felt low. She waited on customers at the Cut Above butcher shop that her husband Jasper owned. Jasper always made sure to let her know that he owned it and her, just one of the many reasons that she was depressed. It wasn't the usual things that kept her depressed like being married to an older man she hated who beat her and verbally and sexually abused her. That had mostly become a terrible routine. When any of it happened, she would pretend she was back in Kentucky with her parents, that her father hadn't died, and that her baby had lived just to get through to the next day.

Her mother, Ida, thinking she was doing what was best for her only child, forced Jasper to marry Rachel when she found out she was pregnant. Rachel was still in high school. She knew that her mother had no way of knowing that Rachel would be living in hell and that during one of her many beatings she would have a miscarriage. She could have stood it better had the baby lived. She would have left and took the baby with her back to Kentucky, but after . . . well . . . any idea of a future had quickly faded away. The days became months, and the months became years. Maybe she deserved this for being a stupid teenager and going to his hotel room. She had believed his act because he put on a good one, and she had been, after all, a child. It made her shudder when she recalled what happened to her in his hotel room and what has happened ever since.

Jasper was just like his parents—cut from the same tree of cruelty. Periodically they would come for a visit. His father, Frank, was a lot older than his mother, Emily. He had been a big shot in the KKK during his younger days, and he passed all his hate and evil ways on to his son.

"I don't know why you came to this coon town. How can you live here? Well, I guess it could have been worse. But I would kill you first," Frank had once said. Just the way he said it sent a chill down Rachel's back. She could tell that Jasper believed it too. He would bring it up a lot. He was afraid of his father and the people his father still associated with.

When Jasper finally rebelled, he moved to the Village to rub his father's nose in it. He opened the Cut Above, the butcher shop that had once belonged to an uncle. According to Jasper, Frank had come with some of his friends and beat the crap out of Jasper, even breaking some bones, but Jasper stayed put. Eventually Frank gave up. As bad as Jasper was, Rachel knew his father was even worse by looking at his downtrodden wife, Emily. Rachel tried to talk to Emily alone one time about her son and how cruel he was to her, but Emily didn't want to talk about it. She said he learned it from his father. Then she whispered, "Jasper was the only baby he didn't beat out of me."

The last time they saw Frank alive, he was a very old man. They went to Mississippi to see him. Rachel thought it was because he wanted to see if his father was as ill as his mother said. His kidneys had given out after years of drinking, and his lungs weren't any better from his years of smoking. He had an oxygen tank and went to dialysis throughout the week. About a month later, Emily called and said Frank had died. If Jasper wanted his ashes, he could come get them. There wasn't going to be a funeral. She finally felt free. Jasper also seemed different. Still mean, but he treated her with indifference. She thought maybe with Frank's passing, Jasper would stop trying to be like him.

But now it was a new low. When her father died, he left her five hundred thousand dollars that she had put in a bank account in Big Rapids. She didn't tell Jasper about the money, thinking that someday soon she would finally get up the nerve to leave, and now she had money. For a glimmer of the moment, she thought of how she could escape Jasper and go back to Kentucky and live a better life. But it was only a glimmer because Jasper was going through her purse one day looking for a pen and found the letter from the attorney. He made her take the money out of the bank and give it to him. First he took away her baby, and now he took away her chance at a new beginning. She was so depressed that she felt like beating Jasper to it and killing herself.

CHAPTER 6

I was feeling a bit better about things now. I have always felt a euphoria when I come here. Whatever worries or troubles that I had in the city would evaporate once I got to the Enchanted Village. Maybe it was enchanted. I don't know, but I just knew I was feeling a lot better because I was here. Although the days were now getting longer, it still got dark around six. I decided I would treat ourselves for dinner. "I think I'll go next door and get us some burgers," I said to Aunt Mae and Uncle James.

"That would be nice, Billie. Tell them we said hi," Aunt Mae said as she looked up from a show we had been watching.

"Will do." I grabbed my hat and coat and headed out the back. I paused and looked at the last of winter on the lake. During the days, spring pushed away the dreary clouds and invited sunshine to take over the skies. At night, it promised that fireflies and crickets would soon make their appearance. I could see little purple and yellow crocuses peeking up through the slushy snow. I always marveled at how beautiful the lake was. I started walking down to where the lake and land met. I passed the stacked beach chairs and tables and the overturned aluminum boats that would provide a good time for all who would soon be using them.

I thought of all the wonderful times that I had been part of in the past years. How beautiful it always was in the summer. Each white table had four matching white chairs. Each table held a pretty colorful umbrella. They had been shades of all the brightly colored baskets of flowers that Aunt Mae nurtured all those late springs, summers, and early falls for decades. Children would be splashing and laughing and making memories that would last their whole lifetime. People swam out to the colorful buoys that marked the shallows and kept them from getting to near drop-off or out where the speedboats and jet skis raced by. People ate, drank, played cards, or just talked to each other. Everyone enjoyed this place.

Well, not everyone. Pig Slop couldn't figure out why I kept wanting him to come for a visit. I just knew once he had been here, he too would be under the Village spell. When he relented and finally came for a day trip last summer, he kept hitting himself like the mosquitoes were only bothering him. He didn't want to be included and sat there quietly. Although many politely tried to draw him into their conversation, they eventually gave up. When he did say something, it was mostly about how much better it was at the Embassy Suites and in the city. He actually tried to drum up business. And it was obvious that he didn't like the McGuires, and they equally didn't like him.

Why had I not seen him for what he was? I had foolishly been taken in by his charm; he could lay it on thick when he wanted to. He was all the snobby stereotypes that I somehow missed seeing. He wore nice suits and expensive cologne. Once a week, he would take me to a nice restaurant in his fancy convertible. Always on a Tuesday. I found out during my sulking period from one of my coworkers (or should I say ex-coworker) that Tuesdays were when his wife had night school, and the kids stayed next door at their grandparents' house. The apartment that I thought he lived in belonged to a friend, so that is how he fooled me for almost a year.

I blew out air, shook my head to shake out the Pig Slop cobwebs, and walked over to the Water's Edge Tavern. Because it was still cold, the open-aired access that I normally walked through was closed. I had to go through the side door. I walked through and saw several locals having some of their last hurrahs before the end of spring season kicked off. I waved hi to all of them.

The neat thing is the McGuires always held a New Season Celebration at the Water's Edge. Everyone from the Village came, and it was a great time. I tried to come every year. It was coming up soon, so I was looking forward to it.

I made my way back to the far end of the bar and saw John on the other end behind the bar talking to a couple. He had a towel hanging over his shoulder. I shed my coat and draped it and my purse over the back of the empty stool next to me. I sat down and looked around. Nothing had changed, and that was the beauty of this place and many businesses like it. It was timeless. Some of the people I knew came over, and we caught up on nothing. I loved it here.

We laughed and then made promises to see each other later. As they walked back to their table, John walked over to me. John was older than Georgie by a year. He had tried marriage almost a year ago, but his wife couldn't take the simple life in the Village. She left him after six months. He was crushed. I only met her at the wedding and didn't really feel she was right for John. Some are just not made for this life. They couldn't do without the malls, movie theaters, fast food, and lots of people whom they didn't know. Tony, who was the same age as Georgie, had escaped marriage, much to his mother's dismay. She wanted grandbabies, and John had been so bitten it didn't look like he was going to give them to her.

Both John and Tony were drop-dead gorgeous. Girls loved them. You could tell they were brothers and were a cross between Terrence Howard and Michael B. Jordan. Yes, that gorgeous. They both had that five o'clock shadow growing on their faces. John kept his hair cut close, and Tony wore his long and sometimes in a ponytail. I always teased Tony about someday having a comb-over and a gray ponytail. I got supreme pleasure whenever John and Tony would skip out of a date to hang out with me and Georgie. Of course, they could be very hard on the guys we dated too. There were many a time when the gas had been siphoned out of our dates' boat or their car tires suddenly lost air. We had all attended college. John and Tony both graduated from Michigan State. Georgie went to Grand Valley State, and I got my hospitality management degree at Ferris State.

"Hi, John." He lifted the hinged counter and walked up to me. I stood up and we embraced.

He gave me a squeeze and said, "You look great, but you always do." I searched his face for the boy I knew. I saw it there when he smiled.

"You big flirt! What's going on?" He was still smiling and shrugged his shoulders.

"Nothing much, Billie. Saw your little red bug this morning. Glad to see you so early in the season," he said as he looked around to make sure everyone had something in their glasses. He then lifted the hinged counter and went back behind the bar. He lowered his voice and leaned over the bar so that we were eye to eye. "Sorry to hear about your ex." Wait a minute. I just got here. How did he find out? . . . Georgie! I shook my head and rolled my eyes. I was going to have to have a talk with her.

"Boys are dirtbags."

"Girls are slimeballs."

We both started to laugh because that is what we always said when we were kids.

"Where's Uncle Pete? I'm used to seeing him in his favorite booth," I said, looking around.

"Dad snuck out for some ice cream at the Big Dipper. He loves that raspberry chip in the waffle cone. He has to sneak out to get it because Mom has been trying to keep him on a diet." That ice cream was homemade and had to be a sin; it was so good. "Did you just drool?" John smiled and asked. I reached up and felt my face. Then I gave him the side-eye.

"Very funny." I'm not going to say that drooling over the Big Dipper's ice cream was out of the question. I've had a steady love affair with it all my life. "How is Aunt Birdie? I need to go see her. She promised me one of her camel cakes the next time I was in town, so I'm going to take her up on it. I love her camel cake." No, it wasn't really a camel baked in a cake or even shaped like a camel. It was really caramel fudge frosting, but when I was little, I called it "camel cake," and the name stuck. All of us call it that now. What can I say—I was cute.

"She's fine. Camel cake." He was really smiling big on that. "She heard you were back, and when I was over to see her earlier, she had just put two in the oven. I assume one was for you. We better get the other one, or I'm coming over to get yours."

"Oh no you're not. Yummy, I can't wait. Hey, how come you're behind the bar? Where's Tony?" John preferred running the kitchen. He ran a tight ship, and his menu was always delicious. He cooked the best gourmet burgers around. He loved to come up with new tasty combinations. He had a full-time cook named Roger who worked for him.

"He got all cleaned up and smelling good and left out of here in a hurry. I don't know what's going on with him lately. He has been doing that a lot. I'm thinking it's a girl." He said "girl" like he was a preteen and wrinkled up his face.

I laughed at his "girl" response and asked, "Who do you think it is? A local? You didn't ask him?" Hmmm. I started going through possibilities around here. I didn't like any of my guesses for Tony.

"You know I don't pry in Tony's love life. When or if he wants to talk about it, I'm sure he will." He waved to a customer who had just walked in and joined a table of laughing people. They had a pitcher of beer on the table and poured their new friend a brew. John made sure the new guy wasn't looking around for service before he turned his attention back to me.

"I guess you're right. By the way, I want to order a carryout." I gave John my order. I didn't need to look at a menu even though John was always trying something new. "I can't wait for this year's celebration. I missed last year, but I won't miss any from now on.

"We have something extra planned." Before I could grill him on it, he held up his hand and said, "Don't even ask. I have been sworn to secrecy." I could tell he wasn't going to spill, so I thought of another way to get that intel.

"Where's Tory? I didn't see her when I came in." Tory was one of the waitresses. Tory was a young, athletic, pretty brown-skinned local girl. She was close to six feet tall in her bare feet and had played basketball through college. She almost made the Olympic team in the 2014 games in Sochi, but an injury to her knee crushed those dreams. She had a smart mouth too. I guess you needed that when you worked in a bar. She also liked to gossip.

"She took the night off too. Said she had something to do. Pretty short notice. Before you try to grill her, she doesn't know what we are doing." John smiled, and then he left to go back to the kitchen through the swinging doors to get the order going. He was back in a few minutes, spied some new customers coming up to the bar, and held up a "wait a sec" finger to me as he went over to them to get their drink order.

I was still going through all the possible girls that Tony could be dating. Now I had to add Tory. Nah! I pretty much canceled her and all the rest of my list of possibilities for all kinds of reasons: too tall, too old, too . . . well, I couldn't think of any that would be a good match. But who's to say it was someone in the Village? Tony had that big Range Rover that he burned up the road in. Maybe it was someone I didn't know. I already didn't like her. By this time, John had returned, and I don't know why, but I felt a bit sour.

"I think you and me should form a club. We can call it the Broken-Hearted Club. We didn't do very well with our love life. Oh, sorry, John, if this is too heavy a conversation. I thought I could talk about it since my recent humiliation was . . . well. . ."—I kind of did that nervous-laugh thing—"more recent." I wouldn't hurt John for the world.

"No problem. I don't think about her every hour anymore," he said with a sad smile. "I guess I keep trying to figure out where I went wrong. I love her . . . loved her." He made that slip of the tongue, and I thought, *Oh geesh, am I going to be stuck like that with Pig Slop? Nope, I'm pretty sure I hated Pig Slop now. Unstuck!* I carefully moved on with the conversation.

"I thought I loved Pig Slop too"—he smiled at "Pig Slop"—"but I keep going over in my mind, how could I have loved anyone who didn't love this place? It is such a part of my chemical makeup. Funny, I love my family and did love my life in the city before it crashed and burned, but I have always loved this place the best. Maybe this is my destiny. Maybe this is my world. Maybe this is why you stay and maybe why she left. Maybe—"

"I need a drink for the rest of this conversation," he said, finishing my "maybe" rhetoric. I guess I was being too serious for John. Although John was as straight an arrow as you would like, he had really taken it hard when his wife left him. He started drinking and smoking his Kools a bit heavier. Aunt Birdie would chastise him, but Uncle Pete said he must ride this thing out for himself. At least that's what Georgie told me.

John gave me one of his lazy smiles. He was really handsome and so sweet. He deserved someone who would make him happy and someone who would love his world here. I watched him as he stood straight up and reached for a shot glass and then turned and looked at me with a questioning look. I nodded my head, and he made it two shot glasses. He put them both down on the bar in front of us and poured himself a shot of dark Bacardi rum and gave me a shot of Jack Daniel's. "So I guess we have formed a weird club," he said with another one of his sweet smiles.

"I guess so." We held up our shot glasses and then clinked them together in wordless cheers and downed them. He refilled them both, and we downed those too. Just then, Roger pushed through the swinging kitchen door and made his way toward me and John.

"Hi, Rog."

"Hi, Billie. Good to see you so early in the season. I put plasticware in the bag. I snuck three pieces of chocolate cake in there for you, Aunt Mae, and Uncle James. They came from the Eats and Sweets. Yummy!" All the kids called my uncle and aunt Uncle James and Aunt Mae. Then he pretended to whisper, making a pointy finger behind the palm of his other hand in John's direction. "Don't tell the boss," he whispered out loud. We all laughed. He put the bag on the counter in front of me and went back into the kitchen. The aroma was sensational.

I reached into my purse and pulled out some cash, but John shook his head. I dug down in the bottom of my purse and pulled out some lint and a shiny quarter. "Don't spend it all in one place." I made a big showing of putting both in the tip jar. John laughed at that. Then I pulled out a proper tip and put that in. "Well, I guess I better get going. Good night, John," I said as I started collecting my things.

"Good night, Billie." He watched me as I left. I could feel his eyes on me, and I turned around. He wiggled his fingers in a goodbye motion, and then he went over to his other customers. I stepped out into the night. It was a bit darker now. I stopped in my tracks. I thought I saw something move in the shadows down by our boathouse. I squinted my eyes and strained to look but didn't see anything. I started down in that direction and felt unseen eyes on me. Thinking it was probably no one or worse, a skunk, I turned and walked in the direction of the Inn. My mind had drifted on to chocolate and camel cake.

CHAPTER 7

I got up and took a nice, long shower. I was so glad to be here and felt this was probably where I should have been anyway. Don't get me wrong, I love my family, but it was long overdue for me to grow up and leave the nest. If I had married Pig Slop (shudder), I would have exchanged one nest for another, and a wife and two children. I guess I didn't know what I was missing by not trying it on my own. Okay, I know, I'm not really on my own, and I am nesting with my Aunt Mae and Uncle James, but I did leave the city, and I'm not looking back unless they kick me out for some reason. Sometimes I'm a lost ball in high weeds.

I ate another delicious breakfast with Aunt Mae and Uncle James, but to tell you the truth, even after having that scrumptious chocolate cake that Rog "snuck" in the bag last night, I was still dreaming of camel cake. I started to wash the dishes, but Aunt Mae shooed me out of the kitchen. I told her about the camel cake last night, and I guess it was on her mind too.

I pulled on my coat and headed over to the McGuires' home. It was such a beautiful day, bright and sunny, and it had warmed up enough that you couldn't see your breath. The McGuires lived on the lake and within walking distance, so I set out on foot. I walked past our wooden sign and gave it a salute. Yes, I was glad to be here. I turned left out of our driveway and onto the street. Nowhere in the Village was a sidewalk. We all walked on the street. As I started past the Water's Edge, I noticed there was a Pepsi truck sitting in the driveway. I saw Tony talking to the driver. I took in a deep breath and broke into a smile. I watched as Tony and the driver fist-bumped, and then Tony saw me. I wiggled my fingers at him but kept walking. I still didn't know how I felt about him having a love life. I don't know why it bothered me, but it did. I saw him say something to the driver, and they both looked my way. I stuck my tongue out at them. Then they both started laughing. I heard Tony say, "Talk to you later, Dillon." The driver got back in his truck and started backing out. I kept walking and jumped out of the way when the truck got a little too close.

"Hey, you gonna go by without speaking?" I could hear crunching of gravel as Tony caught up with me and started walking beside me. "I haven't seen you since Thanksgiving, and you left then in a big hurry. You going to give me a proper hug?" We both stopped. He opened his arms, and I moved into them. He felt warm and tingly, or maybe that was me. I could smell the fresh scent of his soap. Then I remembered he had this mystery girlfriend and pushed him away. He looked disappointed.

"You could've always come visit me. But didn't," I said sarcastically and started walking again. Tony kept pace beside me.

"Hello, you had a man, if you could call him that. The sleaze." Obviously tele-Georgie had been keeping everyone informed, including Tony. "Where are you going in such a hurry? You can't stop for a minute and talk to me?"

"I'm on a mission." I kept walking and then reached up and brushed my hair out of my face.

"On a mission? Where to?"

"It's a secret mission." I wasn't going to share my cake with either John or Tony. I knew I would have to share it with Aunt Mae and Uncle James, but I was sure I would get the lion's share out of our threesome.

"Oh. It wouldn't have anything to do with the retrieval of a top-secret-formula camel cake, would it?" He chuckled. I stopped in my tracks and looked at him in surprise. "Not really a secret mission, Ms. James Bond. Mom called me this morning and said if you hadn't come by before noon for me to deliver the cake to you."

"I love your mom. Georgie is going to be so jealous that she missed it. You know I'm going to rub it in." Serves her right for blabbing. I started walking again and Tony kept pace. "I know the way. Are you just going to follow me?"

He broke into a big smile. "I just wanted to tell you that I'm glad you are here and . . . I really hope you decide to stay this time. I missed you." Then he turned around and headed back in the direction of the Water's Edge.

I don't know why I did it, but I turned around and yelled to him, "*Tell your secret girlfriend that!*" Aha, my life wasn't the only one discussed. It was Tony's turn to stop in his tracks. He turned and then caught up with me. He moved around in front of me and started walking backward so that he could face me.

"Why you always so mean to me, Billie? You *must* love me. I have always loved you." He made a pulsing heart out of his hands in front of his chest. I smiled and rolled my eyes. He's so full of . . . himself. Ha, you thought I was going to say something else. Well, that too.

"I *must* go get my camel cake." Then I stepped around him and stepped up my pace.

Tony stopped and watched as Billie walked away and shook his head. He blew his chance to say what he wanted to say to her. He was still watching her walk up the street until Mr. Ross, the owner of the town's Ace Hardware, honked as he drove by in his truck. It woke Tony abruptly out of his thoughts. Mr. Ross, never stopping, slowed down and lowered his window as he passed by and said, "Nice day, huh, Tony? Spring is fighting to take over. Snow will be all gone before you know it."

Tony returned the wave. "Hey, Mr. Ross. How's it going? Yup, nice day." As the truck headed on up the road, Tony turned and went inside the Water's Edge.

I walked up to the McGuires' backdoor and knocked. I looked around the backyard and saw all Aunt Birdie's pretty decorative bird feeders filled with happy chirping birds. Uncle Pete always complained about how there was always bird poop all around, but he and his boys were the ones who gave them to her. It made her happy. I could hear Aunt Birdie as she approached the door. She opened it, and her face lit up the moment she saw it was me.

"Billie, I am so glad to see you. Come on in." She opened the door up wide. I walked in.

"Hi, Aunt Birdie. I am so glad to be here." Aunt Birdie was beautiful, and I could see her son's faces in her face. She walked almost everywhere, and she stayed fit. She and Uncle Pete played a lot of golf and tennis now that John and Tony have taken over the Water's Edge. They both looked younger than their years. They had a very good life here and it showed.

We hugged each other and did our air kisses. Aunt Birdie, still holding on to me, stepped back and looked me over.

"You have grown into such a beautiful woman, Billie. We are so glad you are back and hope you will stay this time. How's your family? Are they going to come this summer?"

"They are well, and they may take this summer off since I will be here."

"That will be different for them, but the Inn will be in good hands. Have a seat. Sit, sit, sit."

I sat down at the kitchen table and looked around. I have spent a lot of time in this house. It is almost as familiar to me as my own. The McGuire home was beautiful. Not magazine beautiful, a truer homey beautiful. Aunt Birdie loved cardinals, and her kitchen reflected it. They were everywhere from salt and pepper shakers to dishes to artwork to oven mitts. They made her kitchen look so inviting. There was a light aroma of cake in the air that made my mouth water.

"Now what brings you here?" she said with a straight face. "It couldn't be the camel cake, could it?" She smiled and went over to a counter where she had a white cardboard cake box that was tied up with string. "You girls were so cute when you were little. I love my boys to death, but I sure missed having little girls to play with and dress up until you and Georgie came along. That darn toilet seat was always up." She laughed again. "I was hoping for granddaughters and still hope for them, but those boys of mine aren't cooperating." Her face clouded over a little. "I worry about John. His heart sure was broken and he hasn't been himself since before Elaine left. Whoever comes along next better be ready for a fight because he isn't going to go willfully," she said with a smile that reached her eyes.

"John will be fine."

"Oh, I know, but it still breaks my heart to see him suffer. I was hoping for that grandchild, so I am suffering too. And I don't have any idea what Tony is doing. He is seeing some mysterious woman. It's all a big 'secret.'" I sure didn't feel very good about this coming from her. I was hoping it was just a rumor, but now I don't know. "I had high hopes for him to settle down with someone of my choosing." We both started laughing at that. "He spends most of his nights at the bar or wherever he is spending them. I know it isn't here. And John has his cottage down the road, so I guess I miss having them around. Even Pete spends most of his time at the bar. But catch me up on your family. How is everyone?" I told her about

Momma and Pops and Georgie and the girls. I pulled out my cell to show her current photos of the girls.

"I can't wait to see them this summer. I will have some little girls to fuss over." She doted on them, and then she got up and beckoned me to follow. "I want to show you something."

CHAPTER 8

We went into the living room. It was just like I remembered it. The
McGuire home always felt like home. I thought again to myself that I
was so glad to be here. Too bad it took a lowlife like Pig Slop to make me
realize what I really wanted all along. Aunt Birdie sat down on the sofa and
patted the cushion next to her. I sat down, and she reached down under
the coffee table and pulled out an old brown leather photo album with gold
swirly designs on it. It had a small rectangular window on the front that
said "Our Family."

"I don't think you have seen a lot of these pictures. I had put this album
in a chest upstairs and just recently found it looking for something else."
She opened it to the first page, and it was Aunt Birdie and Uncle Pete's
wedding announcement. It had a piece of faded lace that must have come
from her dress or veil. The next pages had photos from their wedding and
reception. Uncle Pete was so handsome in his tux. He had lots of hair that
was very black and a thick mustache to match; both are now very gray. John
and Tony may have gotten their looks from their mother, but they both got
their tallness from their father. Aunt Birdie was a beautiful bride. Her dress
was made of white satin and lace with little pearls sewn in throughout. She
wore a long flowing lace veil. If I thought she was tiny now, she was even
more tiny then. They were married at the little village chapel up the road.
There were photographs of the reception after and of their wedding cake
and presents. I even recognized some of the people from the Village in the
photos including Aunt Mae and Uncle James. I pulled my cell out and took
pictures of the photos to show them later.

The next event in the album was a baby announcement for John. We
looked at the next few pages with pictures of Aunt Birdie and Uncle Pete

holding baby John. They looked like kids themselves. Aunt Birdie had even little locks of John's hair. Turning the pages, you could see John as a toddler, and Aunt Birdie was clearly expecting Tony. Then there was the baby announcement for Tony and his baby picture. I touched his photographed chubby baby toes and smiled. Like John, there were also locks of Tony's hair too. I made a promise to myself that I was going to work harder to not argue with him. There was a picture of Georgie and Tony as babies. She was so cute. Aunt Birdie and I both said, "Awwww," at the same time. A couple of pages later there I was. I was adorable too if I must say so! There were a lot of pictures of John and Tony playing in the sand, fishing with their dad or in the lake.

"You and Georgie were such cuties. I thought then one of you would be a perfect match for one of my boys. You are always in our thoughts. I really love this picture of you and Tony." She pointed at a picture where we were obviously at the Big Dipper eating ice cream cones. We had ice cream all over our faces, hair, and clothes. "Did you just drool?" she asked. I laughed and she joined me. Just then we heard the backdoor open and shut.

"Mom, you aren't showing her those old pictures, are you?" Tony walked in carrying a bag.

"Yes, and I saw your naked butt. Shameful!" I said. All of us laughed. I flipped the pages back and showed him his naked baby picture, and we laughed again.

Then Tony said, "Mom, John sent that bag of food you asked for." He then turned to me and said, "I also came home to show you something"—he rolled his eyes—"but it wasn't my naked butt."

"Been there, seen it, bought the T-shirt, 'Saw Tony's Little Naked Butt,'" I said, invisibly reading it across my shirt. Aunt Birdie laughed, and Tony just shook his head.

"Just wait a minute, we are almost at the end of this album," Aunt Birdie said. Tony sat down next to me on the sofa and the three of us crowded together. We looked at the rest of the pictures. Then we revisited the ones Tony hadn't seen with us. We laughed at what we had on and what we were doing, and by the end of the album, we all had nostalgia in our hearts.

"So, what is the big secret thing going on at the Celebration?" Aunt Birdie looked puzzled, and Tony looked guilty. Aha!

"I don't know what you are talking about. What is she talking about, Tony?" Aunt Birdie wanted to know too.

Tony had a firm look on his face and said, "Nun-ya! Both of you will find out in due time." I could tell by the resolve on his face that he wasn't going to tell. "Okay, now can I show her?" Tony said, looking at his mother as he stood up. He rounded the coffee table and waited.

"Yes," she said in a mocking tone, shaking her head, but with a smile that matched Tony's. "Don't forget your cake," she yelled as we were going out the door.

"You don't have to worry about that. I'll come back in and get it," I yelled back.

Tony led me out to their pole barn. Tony opened the door, and we walked in. I was expecting to see Uncle Pete's old blue-and-white pontoon that he had for years, but when Tony turned on the light, there was a brand-new black-and-beige pontoon sitting there. It was beautiful. Tony had a step stool by the boat's door. He helped me up and then followed me. As we walked around, he proudly pointed out all its features. It was top of the line.

"Wow. You are going to let me drive it, aren't you?"

"I don't think so. You're a nut behind a wheel and a speed demon. But, if you give me a piece of Mom's camel cake, a big piece mind you, I might let you sit behind the wheel."

"No deal, boy, you're greedy. You aren't getting any of my camel cake. Nada!" And with that, I climbed down and ran back to the house. "Tony's trying to get some of my camel cake," I yelled out to Aunt Birdie when I came through the door. I didn't see her and almost ran into her in the kitchen.

"He better not. And don't you give any of it to John either. I made two." She handed me the cake box, and I kissed her on the cheek.

"Thanks, Aunt Birdie. And thanks for showing me the photo album. I'm going to send Georgie the pictures I took on my cell of her. She will love them."

"Come back and see me again."

"I will. Bye bye!" Then I went out the backdoor and almost ran into Tony, who had been waiting for me to come out.

"Are you stalking me? Your mom has your cake so stay out of mine."

"Why you so mean, girl? I can carry that for you." I rolled my eyes.

"No thanks. You have ulterior motives."

"Yes, I guess I do," he said with a smile.

CHAPTER 9

Since it was early spring, it was still cold, and there was snow on the ground. There weren't any guests at the Inn. We did have some hardcore guest from time to time who preferred the isolation and no crowds, but they were the exception. We didn't have anyone yet, but the summer months would more than make up for the colder months. The Village wasn't in full swing yet and ran on limited hours. Originally, I thought the whole idea of me coming here was a ruse to get me out of my slump, but after spending a few weeks with my aunt and uncle, I soon found that they really did need me. When we would come and take over the Inn in July it would more or less be a baton handoff between us and them. They would hurry off to catch a flight in the city to wherever they were vacationing, and we would become entrenched in running the Inn. I didn't see that they were aging, but now it was apparent. So I let them relax more and I did the dusting, cleaning, mopping, and most of the chores that they usually did when it was slow. I took reservations, and our bookings through the summer looked very good so far. I even repainted a couple of rooms. Don't get me wrong, I loved it. It was a lot better than my job at the Embassy Suites. I got to do every aspect, not just part.

I think a lot of old towns like ours have people living in them who are a bit eccentric that the locals would call characters. Someone everybody knew. Our character was an old man named Jake Glover, but everyone called him Never Late. He was called that because he seemed to always show up at someone's dinner table right when they were having their meal. As time went on, his nickname had a nickname of Never. Never was a white man in his seventies who seldom shaved (if at all). Although he had mostly white hair, there was a part of it that was brilliant red.

I heard that at some time during his life, he had worked on the pipeline in Alaska where he must have learned how to rough it. He liked his privacy and lived in a remote spot in the woods in an old camper that had seen better days. Who am I kidding—it had seen better minutes. He had electricity but no running water. He lived near the creek that flowed into our lake and had thick woods all around his camper except what he cleared himself. He had a matching dilapidated outhouse too. He was off the grid, one would say.

Never wasn't one to beg, he would gladly work for his meal by doing any odd job that was needed. He came prepared with his own tools and was very handy. One tool he was particularly proud of was a wrench he received on a project he was on that was engraved with "Thank you for your hard work, Governor Jay Hammond." Never loved telling the story of how the governor came in person and handed out the engraved wrenches to each team member. Eventually Never got tired of the long nights or long days or both and moved around from state to state. He finally moved here to the Village. He liked the weather, his freedom, and the people.

I remember one time when I was a kid, a lot of us were at the beach. One of the summer kids was teasing me about seeing a ghost. From the way Pudgy was looking so smug, he must have just told them about it. About then, Never was walking by and said, "Aw. That's nothing. Pudgy here saw Big Foot when he looked down," and then he winked at me. Everybody laughed including me, and Pudgy even laughed too. Like almost everything else in the Village, Never had been here my whole life. I liked Never from then on. I thought of him when I was back in the city at a local Barnes and Noble. I was buying a murder mystery when a book about Alaska caught my eye. I picked it up and glanced through it. It had a lot of beautiful photographs and maps. I thought of Never and bought it for him.

Although it didn't seem to surprise Aunt Mae when Never knocked at the backdoor one morning, it did me. I guess Never had added breakfast to his timely visits. We didn't include meals at the Inn because there were so many other options close by that it didn't make sense, and it also gave the other places business. But Aunt Mae still cooked great meals for us and evidently for Never now and then.

Never walked over and took a seat across from me. He didn't talk much and just kept his eyes down on his empty plate while he waited for Aunt Mae to load it up.

"Jake, would you like your eggs scrambled or over easy?" Aunt Mae was one of the few people in town who called him by his given name. She felt that his nickname and nick-nickname weren't very nice. He didn't seem to mind it, but then again you couldn't tell what was on his mind. A conversationalist he wasn't.

"Over easy if you don't mind," he said without looking up. He was looking at his empty plate so intently that I started looking to see if there was something on it. I think he must have seen a movie or two about a crotchety old man and patterned himself after him. The silence was killing me, and I struggled for something to say. I finally used the standard everyone uses when they can't think of anything else.

"Hey, Nev . . . er . . . a . . . Jake"—I got the side-eye from Aunt Mae— "how do you like this spring weather?" I got up and grabbed the coffee pot. I filled the cup in front of Never. "Would you like cream and sugar?"

"No, thank you, Billie." I was beginning to think that he had not heard my weather question when he said, "I miss the snow in Alaska sometimes." He looked up at me then. "The snow here can get deep, but not like it does in Alaska. It could get awfully cold though. This weather is good." Then he went back to studying his plate. By then Aunt Mae started loading up his plate with food. To his credit, he respectfully waited for us to have our food before he touched any of his. Uncle James had come into the kitchen.

"Hi, Never. How're you doing?" Uncle James never feared the wrath of Aunt Mae. He winked at me and took his seat at the head of the table.

"Okay, James." Never was a real conversationalist.

Aunt Mae brought over filled plates of food to the rest of us and sat down. That must have been the starting pistol shot for Never to jump in. He finished his first plate and was rewarded with a second helping of everything.

"Would anyone like another cup of coffee? I'm about to make another pot."

"Yes, ma'am," Never said.

"Thanks, Aunt Mae. I would like another cup as well," I responded as I looked inside my empty cup.

"Not for me. I gotta get out there and shovel the pathway," Uncle James said as he slid out of his chair and stood up. He reached into his pocket and pulled out a cigar.

"I can do it, Uncle James," I said.

"You need to let someone else do that, James," said Aunt Mae with her back to us. She was busy making coffee. And without looking she added, "And put that cigar away. You know you aren't supposed to be smoking those anymore. Nasty smelly old things. I don't know how you can stand it."

"I can do it for ya," said Never. I watched Uncle James put the cigar back in his pocket.

"That would be very nice, Jake. Thank you," said Aunt Mae.

"Would everyone stop treating me like an old man? I got this." With that, Uncle James pulled the cigar back out of his pocket and put it in his mouth. He left the kitchen.

"I will come back and do it, Mae. I have to help unload a delivery truck at the Pines and Needles, but after that I will come back and shovel the snow. Ain't that much. Just leave a shovel out front for me."

I think that was the most I had ever heard Never say in one sentence. It kind of surprised me. Just then I remembered the book I got him.

"Ah Jake, I have something for you." I ran to get it. I went to my room and pulled my suitcase out of the closet. Not knowing when I would see Never, I left it there. I pulled it out and headed back through the lobby and saw Uncle James. He had put on his heavy coat and knitted cap and was heading out the front door. He still had his unlit cigar hanging out of his mouth. I sighed. He sure was stubborn. I hurried into the kitchen. I handed the book to Never. He examined it carefully like I had just handed him an artifact. I went and got a plastic bag for him to carry it in. He looked up at me when I handed him the bag, and for once I felt like he really looked at me and not through me. His eyes showed true appreciation.

"Thank you." He got up slowly and walked out the backdoor. Through the window I could see him looking into the bag like it was full of gold.

Aunt Mae started running dishwater in the sink and turned around to me and said, "You just made his day." She dried her hands on a piece of paper towel that she just yanked off the roll. "You have to remember that Jake has no one. No one to sing "Happy Birthday" to him. No one to laugh with or hang out with. And no one to give him presents. I know he has more or less done it to himself, but it doesn't change things. He came here when he was a much younger man and didn't care that the town was predominantly black. He treated everyone with respect. He had ideas, many that made the town better. But somewhere and someplace in time, he lost himself." She turned back to the sink and started washing dishes.

I decided at that moment that I would somehow break through Never's barriers and help him find himself. Just because my life was in shambles didn't mean that I couldn't do something for someone else. What could it hurt?

CHAPTER 10

I shooed Aunt Mae out the kitchen and finished doing the dishes. After setting the last one in the drying rack, I decided to go next door to the Water's Edge and see what Tony and John were up to. "I'm going next door, Aunt Mae," I yelled as I put on my hat and jacket and headed out the backdoor.

"Would you check the mailbox for me?" she yelled from some room upstairs in return.

I stopped in my tracks at the backdoor. "Will do," I yelled as I turned and headed to the front door.

I opened the door and ran out the porch. That was where I found Uncle James laying on the sidewalk with a snow shovel clutched in his hands.

I started yelling for Aunt Mae, and it must have been loud enough to bring John running with Tony not far behind him from next door. John called 911, and Tony kept running until he was next to Uncle James. He bent down and gently examined him for a pulse. Then he started doing CPR. Aunt Mae came running too, but I held on to her so that Tony could keep working on Uncle James until the ambulance arrived. John had gone back and got a blanket and covered Uncle James up. We could all hear the siren in the distance getting closer, and when they arrived, they took over from Tony. I could see Uncle James move and that he started breathing on his own. The EMTs quickly put Uncle James under oxygen. They lifted him on a gurney and then into the back of the ambulance. Aunt Mae climbed in with help from the EMTs and asked me to follow the ambulance in my car.

"I don't think you should drive under the circumstances, Billie. I will take you to the hospital. John can run things at the Water's Edge. Stay here while I go get the car," said Tony and quickly ran to get his car.

A few minutes later, he was dispatching me in the passenger seat of his Range Rover. We got to the hospital and found Aunt Mae waiting in the emergency room. She looked terrible and it broke my heart. Tony and I sat down next to her and waited. Tony went to the cafeteria and got us each a cup of coffee. We sat there in shock, all of us holding hands. Finally, they called Aunt Mae's name, and she was led back to where Uncle James was. Tony sat with me with his arm around me and told me that Uncle James was in good hands. Then after what seemed to be hours, a nurse came and took us back to triage. We were given rough directions to the partitioned-off space where Uncle James was. Tony held my hand, and together we walked through the emergency labyrinth. Everywhere we heard beeping, curtains being pulled open and shut, people in scrubs quickly moving here and there in squeaky shoes, and people in some type of pain or agony. When we got to Uncle James, he was still under oxygen but was awake. He waved at me, and through my tears I smiled. I grabbed his hand and held it to my face.

"The doctor said that he's had a mini-stroke, but because of Tony's fast thinking and giving CPR, he would probably be okay with a lot of rest. Thank you, Tony, for saving his life." Her voice cracked. Tony, not knowing what to say, just kind of waved.

"Yes, Tony, thank you," I said with a great big lump in my throat.

"They are going to admit him, and I am going to stay. I want you to go home and get some rest," said Aunt Mae. She looked so fragile that I protested, but I didn't want to add to the strain of the situation, so I let Tony take me home. Tony walked into the Inn with me. We sat together on the sofa in the common room in front of the fireplace. Tony started a fire. Because we had been up into the wee hours of the morning at the hospital with no sleep, I soon drifted off.

I woke up in the same spot to the smell of bacon frying. I had a quilt draped over me, and a roaring fire was burning in the fireplace. It took me a minute to remember that Uncle James was in the hospital. I jumped up and headed toward the kitchen. Tony was there in his bare feet, cooking eggs and bacon. Buttered toast was piled up on a plate, and as I took a deep breath, I could smell the aroma of fresh coffee brewing. There was quite a bit of food for just the two of us.

"Are you cooking for an army?" I asked while yawning at the same time. He turned to me and started to say something when we heard the front door open and slam shut.

"Hello, is anyone here?" It was Georgie. As much as she and I bicker from time to time, I sure was glad she was here.

"We're in the kitchen," I yelled back and then turned to look at Tony.

"John called your mom and dad and Georgie yesterday. He kept them updated." He began pulling bacon pieces out the hot grease and onto a paper-toweled plate. Georgie had made it back to the kitchen and ran over and hugged me and then hugged Tony. He kissed her on the cheek and patted her on her back. Then moved back to working on his cooking. She swiped a piece of bacon off the plate he was holding and plopped down in the nearest chair.

"Momma and Pops will be here later. Any word on Uncle James?" she said while crunching on the piece of bacon.

"I was just getting ready to call the hospital. He looked so weak. I wish I had shoveled that snow," I said as I reached for a piece of bacon.

"It's all shoveled now. John said that Never came around and finished the job. Me and John will take over that job from now on. It isn't like we haven't done it before, but sometimes Uncle James beats us to it." Tony put the plate of bacon on the table next to the plate of scrambled eggs.

"If I hadn't been on my way to the mailbox, I may not have found him in time, and Tony may not have given him CPR in time and John hadn't—" I started saying.

"But none of that happened, and he is now resting in comfort," Tony interrupted. "Don't invite doom, Billie." Tony was always saying that. "Sit down and have some breakfast. We can call afterwards."

Sounded like a good plan, and besides the food smelled so good. John came over and joined us. It felt like old times with the four of us together. We made short work of Tony's breakfast, and after my second cup of coffee, I reached for my cell and dialed Aunt Mae. She didn't pick up, and it went to her voicemail. I left a message and hung up. John went out the backdoor, probably to have a smoke. Georgie gathered up the dirty dishes and stacked them on the counter next to the sink while Tony started the dishwater. Tony washed and I dried while Georgie updated us on the girls and her husband Marcus's new job. The girls, Jazzy and Minx, were at Marcus's parents so that Georgie could come to the Inn without having to worry about them too. When my phone played the Temptations singing "Can't Get Next to You" ringtone, I picked it up.

"Hi, Aunt Mae, how is Uncle James?" I put it on speaker so that everyone could hear and talk.

"Hi, Billie. He had a fitful night because he was hooked up to all kinds of things, and he hates to sleep on his back. Plus he wants his nasty cigars, but that is over." I could tell she was giving him the stink eye when she said that. "He is looking at me right now. Say hi, honey."

"Georgie and Tony are here, and I have you on the speaker." Of course Uncle James picked the same time to talk, and we overlapped.

"What did you say?" we both said in unison. I hurriedly repeated that Georgie and Tony could hear him.

"I'm feeling fine. Bring me a cigar." You have to give it to Uncle James for trying.

"It's the drugs they have him on, and don't," said Aunt Mae.

"That may be true, but I want my cigar. I am feeling sleepy . . . cigar . . ."

"He just dozed off again. The doctor said he was very lucky. There doesn't seem to be much damage, but they want to run more tests. It could have been worse." We all heard her sniff and knew she had tears in her eyes. "I just don't know what I would do without him."

"Don't worry about anything, Aunt Mae. We will take care of the Inn and anything else that needs to be done. You just worry about Uncle James," Georgie said, and we all agreed.

"The doctor just came in so I have to hang up." And before we could say anything more, she hung up.

The dishes were done, and Tony had to get back to the Water's Edge.

"If you need anything, anything, just call," Tony said to us both.

I walked over to him and hugged him like I wasn't going to let go. "Thank you for everything," I said. The lump in my throat had returned, and I tried not to cry. Tony cradled me and then Georgie joined our hugfest.

"He will be okay. Don't worry," he quietly said. We all stepped back. He grabbed his coat off the coat hook and left out the backdoor.

About an hour later, Momma and Pops arrived. We all hugged, and after they rested a little from their ride, we all piled in the car and went to the hospital. It was good having most of the family together, and it seemed to cheer everyone up. After everyone caught up on what was going on with jobs, kids, and weather, Aunt Mae stood up.

"James and I appreciate all of you being here. Don't we, James?" Uncle James just nodded his head. "And we have been discussing our future

---

43

for when James is released. We have had a lot of good years running the Loving Arms, and we loved it. But we have come to the conclusion that we are just getting too old to continue running it well." She reached for Uncle James hand and grasped it like a lifeline. "We think that it is time that we step aside and turn it over to Billie." The look of shock on my face made Aunt Mae hurriedly go on. "Billie, you have done so much for the Inn since you arrived. You have the talent it takes and also the love of the place to drive you. Georgie can't leave her husband and kids to come help you run it, nor do we think she would want to." She looked over at Georgie who was shaking her head no. "You have our support as to whatever you choose to do. I know I am rambling, but the idea is new to us too."

I had all eyes in the room on me, and I looked at each one of them.

"Billie, you were groomed for this from the time you were a child," Pops said softly as if profound. "Your mother and I never had it in our hearts other than our annual July. But if this is not what you want, speak your mind. Although we have to know soon because people have reservations, if you need a little time to think about it, we understand. If we have to sell the place, we have to sell it."

"I accept," I said so quickly that everyone kind of snapped to attention. That's how I became the new proprietress of the Loving Arms Inn.

CHAPTER 11

The Andersons were three black sisters, Rose, Daisy, and Lily. Folks would sometimes call them the Flowers. They were all in their seventies. Rose was the oldest sister who had moved from Detroit to the Village with her husband, Ralph. Ralph built beautiful handcrafted furniture and made a good living from it. Rose loved to sew, and because of the long winter months, she made quilts while Ralph built furniture. When Ralph died, she stayed on. She made so many quilts that she started selling them. Daisy was widowed as well and living in Detroit. Lily never found someone to settle down with. They both were quilters too. Sometime after Daisy's husband passed, Lily moved in with Daisy.

In the summer, they would come and stay the whole summer with Rose. They loved the easy life of the Village. They got tired of the effects of Jim Crow in Detroit, so in 1968, they joined their sister, Rose, in the Village. Daisy and Lily had their own cottage. They all made a decent living from the sale of their quilts but ended up with loads of fabric odds and ends. They started selling their quilts and odds and ends to the tourists. The owner of the Golden Thimble decided to move in with her son in Texas. The store was already furnished with the right kind of shelving and fixtures, so it was an easy decision to buy it. With it being three of them, one of the sisters would run the store while the other two went to a large supply store in the city. They liked being choosy at what they bought for their store and didn't like ordering without seeing firsthand what they were buying.

That morning, Rose and Daisy did the shopping. As Never approached the shop, they were just pulling in. "Good morning, Never," both ladies shouted out to him as they climbed out of both sides of the truck.

"Good morning, Miss Rose, Miss Daisy," he responded as he let down the tailgate of their truck and started to unload. He did this often enough to know where they wanted the things to go.

"We are going to have spaghetti tonight for dinner if you want to stop by," Daisy said as she walked toward the door to the store. No one wanted to have Never feel cheated. He was a good worker of all the odds and ends that left others to do something else. She opened the door and walked inside.

"We are having a forty-year anniversary celebration at the church this Sunday. We would be glad to hold you a seat next to us. There will be a big Sunday dinner after services too," said Rose as she walked toward him. "Lots of good food, Never." Not giving him time to answer, she turned and headed in the same direction as her sister. "Just think about it." Rose knew Never wouldn't come for his own reasons, but she always asked. She had a warm spot in her heart for Never. She knew him before he had become a recluse, when he was younger and had first come to the Village. She felt a secret joy whenever he was around. She knew he was a bit on the eccentric side, but there was something under all that hair, beard, and gruffness that she was attracted to. She didn't even tell her sisters how she felt since he never made any indication of feeling anything for her.

"Thank you, Miss Rose." Never stayed away from churches. The Lord had let him down. Nope, he had no use for church. Never continued to unload the Andersons' truck when he heard a large vehicle go by. Jasper Pennington, who owned the Cut Above butcher shop, was driving by in his truck when he saw Rose and Never. He almost passed them, so he had to back up a bit. His truck was one of those big ones that made a rumbling sound that got louder as he accelerated. It sat on jacked-up tires. Didn't know how he was able to climb up in it all the time.

"Hey, Rose," he yelled out of the passenger window that he just slid down. Some Willie Nelson song was blaring out his radio. "There was an ambulance over at the Inn. They're saying that old man James had a stroke. His niece found him laying in the snow. You old girls better get someone to shovel your snow. You don't want to end up dead in the snow." He then turned and looked at Never. It was not a surprise to Never that Jasper had not acknowledged him. He had always treated Never with disgust. He told Never one time that he didn't know why he would have come here back when it was almost all black and preferred being around black people more than his "own kind." His own kind. If Jasper was an example of "his own kind," Never didn't want any part of it. "Gotta run," Jasper said, burning some rubber as he drove off.

"My word," said Rose. "That truck will be the death of that man." Never hoped it was. He didn't like Jasper. Jasper was a forty-something white man and moved to the Village from Mississippi. Around that time, the Village had become more diverse, meaning there were a large number of white residents who saw a good thing and moved in. They were mostly good people and not of the same opinion as Jasper. Jasper had been taught prejudice well by his parents. Jasper was a good-looking man, but he had a way of talking down to everyone, calling the Andersons "you old girls." Never felt sorry for his wife, Rachel. She was real frail-looking. She was barely in her twenties but looked older than she was. Being married to Jasper probably aged her. She hardly ever left the house except to work at the butcher shop.

"That's so sad about James. I hope he gets better. I'll pray for him," said Rose, nodding her head.

"I'll shovel your walk, Miss Rose, after I empty the truck."

"Thank you, Never," she said. She started to say something else but changed her mind. She turned and went into the shop.

Never felt really bad about James Rivers. He felt like it had been his fault since he didn't shovel the snow right away, but he had promised the Anderson sisters that he would help them unload their truck. It didn't stop him from feeling bad, though. Especially after Billie had been so nice by giving him the book. He had forgotten what it was like to have someone give him something that was just for him. He knew that most people thought he was a funny old man. He hadn't minded it, and he actually liked his nickname. He didn't fault the people of the Village if they didn't reach out to him. He didn't want to be close to anyone again.

As a boy, he had grown up near the Enchanted Village. He had known a lot of the boys his age from the Village. He would often come over to the lake to fish or swim with them. He didn't feel they were any different just because they had different-colored skin. They didn't treat him any different either. He worked for the U.S. Forestry when he got out of school and met a girl from Los Angeles named Susan, who had been visiting friends. He followed her out there and married her. He never liked it out there. He missed the snow and tried to talk Susan into moving to Michigan. They had a little boy named Travis by then, and she wanted to be around her family. They had a lot of arguments about it and eventually grew apart. He tried to hold his marriage together for his son's sake, the one person that he truly loved, but he felt miserable. Her family treated him like he wasn't good enough because he liked to work outside. All those years with the forestry made it hard for him to work inside. He switched jobs a lot trying to find something he liked to do in LA. In the seventies, he saw where they were building a pipeline in Alaska and decided he had tried long enough and left for that adventure. He still remembers the look on his son's face when he left. His leaving didn't mean he didn't love the boy, but he felt his staying would only make things harder for him. Susan divorced him shortly after he left.

Never loved Alaska. It reminded him of his home in Michigan. He lived around the indigenous people in Alaska, and it verified for him that people, no matter what color, are basically the same. He learned a lot about living under harsh conditions, and he welcomed it. He wanted that punishment for letting his son down. After years in Alaska, Never traveled around the states but decided to settle in the Village. It was still mostly black then, and some of his boyhood friends were still there. He had been to LA a few times to visit his son, but by then Travis had outgrown his absent father. Never didn't blame him; he blamed himself for letting the boy down. Then one day, a letter that had been chasing him all around finally caught up with him. It was from his ex-wife, Susan. She told him Travis had been in a terrible car accident and had died. His world stopped, and he was mad at God. He just crawled up inside himself and tried to die too. When he didn't die, he just took the days as they came. He couldn't bring himself into talking to anyone, and he only told one person about the day his life stopped. So every time Miss Rose would ask him to come to church, he just couldn't.

But now, Billie had given him a book, and it cracked open the rusty gate to his heart. Just a crack, mind you, but enough that he felt different. Better. Even after he heard about James and the dark clouds of guilt came rolling back, he still felt "different." Mae and James had always been good to him, but maybe having someone young like Billie giving him a present reminded him of his son. Never was a complex man.

"Never, would you mind going over to the Cut Above and picking up an order for me? Seeing Jasper reminded me of it," Rose yelled out from the open backdoor. "Just ask him for it. I called it in yesterday."

"Yes, Miss Rose. I'll go get it." In Never's mind, it was a bad day when he saw Jasper once, but now he is going to have to see him again? But for Miss Rose, he was happy to do anything for her. Well, anything but go to church.

CHAPTER 12

After he was done shoveling the Andersons' walkway, he walked over to the Inn. The shovel was leaning against the porch. He could see where James had been laying and all the footprints of everyone else who had stood around him. He felt bad again and started shoveling. When he finished, he put the shovel back where he had found it and headed for the Cut Above.

Most of the main businesses were within walking distance—well, what Never felt was walking distance. He didn't know what he would have to carry, so he decided to drive. He had an old truck that he kept running somehow. It had a lot of rust, burned oil, and spit out a lot of smoke, but it got him around. He pulled into the gravel parking lot of the Cut Above. The truck door groaned as he opened it and groaned when he slammed it shut. His footsteps crunched in the gravel, and he dodged the potholes that were filled with melted ice and snow. The weather was changing, getting warmer. By next week, if it didn't snow again, all the snow should be gone.

Never yanked the butcher shop door open, and he heard the tinkle of the bell over the door. The butcher shop always had a smell to it. Not a bad one like spoiled meat but a smell. There were a few customers, all people he knew, standing in line, patiently waiting for Jasper's wife, Rachel, to take their orders. Never didn't see Jasper.

"Hi, Never, how ya' been?" asked Zander Green. He was a black man who had a beautiful cottage with a lot of land on the lake. He and his wife Joyce took great pride in their home, and it showed.

"Hi, Never, have you heard about poor James Rivers? We were just talking about it," said Linda Freeman. She went on with her chatter, and Zander added comments every now and then. Linda was a white lady whose husband had a boat repair business in the Village. Mixed marriages were a common thing in the Village. People in the Village had long ago learned how people were all the same even when they looked different on the outside. That is, all except Jasper.

"Hi. I just saw him this morning. Sad." Never then looked out of the window so that they wouldn't try to talk to him more. Zander and Linda went on with their conversation.

Thinking about Jasper, Never wondered where he was. Rachel wordlessly worked away cutting meat and then weighing it. Then would come the sound of paper being ripped off the roll to wrap up the orders. Every now and then, Never would say, "Yup" or "Nope" to Zander and Linda, but his thoughts were not with their chatter. He looked at Rachel, and he felt sorrow. She had married a man over twice her age. She looked tired and like she was just going through the motions. No one knew very much about her, and they were very surprised when Jasper came back from the city with a child bride. That's what all the folks called her behind his back. No one would dare say anything to his face. He was an explosive type. Anything would and did set him off.

Zander and Linda started heading to the door with their packages in their hands. The little bell tinkled again as they pushed open the door, and they could still be heard talking about James as the door closed behind them. Rachel looked over at Never and said, "Hi, Never, what can I get for you today?" She had a bit of a Southern accent. Never had heard she was from somewhere in Kentucky.

"I've come to pick up for Miss Rose," he said as he walked up closer to the counter. Rachel put both hands on the counter and did a little stretch like she was trying to remove an ache in her back.

"It's in the back," she said as she kind of winced.

"Are you okay?" Never surprised himself by asking. He tried to stay away from people's miseries.

"Yeah, I guess I'm just a bit tired. I'm going to go see my momma in Louisville. I can't wait to get away . . ." She left words unsaid that said it all. She kind of looked around. "I don't know where Jasper is. Mrs. Anderson has a pretty large order for some church function, and the box is a bit heavy. Would you mind coming back later when he's here? Oh shoot, I just broke the chain on my locket." She pulled it from her neck and opened the register. She missed the register and it dropped on the floor. Rachel started to bend down to retrieve it but before she could, Never got to it first. He picked it up and handed it to her. She put it in the open register.

"You just show me where it is, Miss Rachel, and I will go get it." Never didn't want to be there when Jasper was there, but he heard Jasper's truck pull in. Rachel looked relieved. She started for the back and beckoned Never to follow. They went into a walk-in cooler. She pointed up to a large box that was sitting on a wire shelf. Never started to walk around her, reaching up to get the box.

"Get your filthy hands off my wife!" Jasper raced in and grabbed Never by his clothes and dragged him out of the cooler.

Rachel was yelling after him, "Stop, Jasper! He was just getting Mrs. Anderson's box," but Jasper was too enraged to hear. By then, Mrs. Baits, who had just parked, was getting out of her car. Jasper yelled a litany of cuss words at Never and then threw him out of the store. The little bell made an awkward type of noise as Never fell backward as he was thrown from the doorway. Never tried to grab anything to break his fall and found empty air. He landed on the ground on his back, just missing Mrs. Baits. "I was just trying to—"

Jasper, now outside, interrupted, "I know what you were trying to do. If I catch you anywhere near my wife again, I'll kill you." Jasper turned and went back into the store. Never could hear Rachel screaming and crying and then nothing. Mrs. Baits checked to see if Never was okay before venturing into the store. Never got up and checked to see if he had been hurt. He seemed to be okay, so he got into his truck. He headed back to his camper. Miss Rose was going to have to get her own order. He was never coming back.

"Oh my goodness. You will never guess what just happened." Mrs. Baits came running into the Bait Shop visibly upset.

Sandy was sitting on a box of canned goods, scrolling through her phone. That stupid Suzy was restocking the candy by the register. Sandy finally remembered her name. She scowled as she heard Ms. Goody Two-Shoes ask, "Are you okay?" Of course she was okay. *She came flying in here like a track star*, thought Sandy.

"I went over to the Cut Above to get my pork chops for tonight's dinner. I like to bread them with crushed club crackers, you know, and then deep fry them to—"

"Would you get on with the story?" Sandy interrupted impatiently. Who cares about how she cooks pork chops? *Boy, do I have to get out of this town*, she thought to herself.

"Well, as I pulled up, I was almost knocked down by Never. Jasper threw him out of his store. I never saw him so mad before in my life. He was yelling at poor old Never, telling him to stay away from his wife, and she was crying . . . that was awful. But then Jasper went inside. I looked to see if Never was okay, and all of a sudden, Rachel quit crying and yelling. I ran inside, and Jasper must have hit her because she was standing there holding the side of her cheek. I yelled at Jasper, and he said she fell. She said she fell too, that she must have tripped on something, but I think he hit her. Well, I yelled at Jasper to just go someplace and cool off. Out he went, and I heard him screech off in his truck." Mrs. Baits took a deep breath and then continued, "She had a red cheek, and I went in the back for some ice. She told me that she was okay, and it was a good thing she was leaving for a week to be with her momma. Then she started crying. Said when she lost the baby everything went bad. I feel so sorry for her." Mrs. Baits went behind the register and opened it. She started counting money and then lifted the till and took out some checks and put them in a canvas bag. "I've got to go to the bank. What a day!"

Interesting, thought Sandy. *Very interesting.* She started a text.

"Sandy! Get off that phone and go help Suzy with the restocking if there's no customers." About then someone came in, and Mrs. Baits started telling the story over again. Sandy finished her text and sauntered over to the register. She wasn't no slave. Let Suzy do the work. She looked over at Suzy, who had just finished stocking the candy. *She was a pretty girl about mid-twenties*, thought Sandy. Her black hair made her look more pale. She came out of nowhere. One day, she showed up and asked the old lady for a job. She said she had been homeless. Probably just got tired of working the streets. Mrs. Baits fell for her story and hired her.

Throughout the entire day, Sandy listened to Mrs. Baits tell every customer the same old story. *I bet she wouldn't be doing all that talking if Jasper came in*, she thought. At least she told the same story each time. By the end of Sandy's shift at the store, she was sick to death hearing about it.

Jasper was fuming. "You trying to make me the laughingstock of this town with that bum?" he screamed. They were standing in their bedroom, and Rachel had been applying ice to her now-bruised cheek. Jasper was oblivious to the pain that he had inflicted on her.

"I tried to tell you, he was just helping me get the box down for Miss

Rose." Rachel had cried all she could cry and had reached a turning point. "When I go to my mother's I'm not coming back."

"Good, I don't want you back," he sneered and started to walk out of the room.

"I'm taking my inheritance money too." Jasper felt a little unsure of himself then. He couldn't let that go. He had plans of his own for that money. He slowly turned around and glared at her.

"Let me make this clear. You are not taking one cent of that money with you. I'm your husband and have rights." He walked over to her and got in her face. She thought for sure he was going to hit her again.

"Keep the money. You took the only thing that mattered to me. Our baby. I just want to go home. I'm tired, and I haven't been well." Jasper smiled and then walked out of the room. Rachel thought she had no tears left, but one silently rolled down her cheek. She began packing.

CHAPTER 13

It had been a few hours since his encounter with Jasper. Never was so upset he forgot to let Miss Rose know that he didn't pick up her box. He didn't own a phone. He put his coat back on and started out of his camper. He thought he heard something, but when he looked around, he didn't see anything. He walked over to his truck, and that's when he saw some footprints by his truck that he knew weren't his. He looked around some more. It kind of creeped him out. He was worried that it may be Jasper coming back to make good on killing him. That made him get in his truck quickly and drive off to the Pines and Needles.

Someone had been there all right and had been watching.

Never pulled into the Pines and Needles. They also had a little bell that jingled when the door was open. All three sisters looked up from their different spots around the store. There were customers sprinkled throughout the little store. Rose was behind the desk, Daisy was looking through some quilt magazines, and Lily was pulling out bolts of fabrics and showing them to a customer.

"Oh, Never, I am so sorry to hear what happened at Jasper's. Josephine called me and told me all about it," Rose said as Never walked toward her. "I feel like I was responsible for all of this." Rose looked so concerned that Never felt bad for her.

"Miss Rose, it's okay. It wasn't your fault. I just came by to tell you that I didn't get your box," he said. He took a deep breath and went on to say, "I'm sorry, but I'm never going to go there again."

"Don't worry about it. I will get it myself. I don't want you to go anywhere close to that crazy Jasper." She softly touched him on his sleeve. "You are a good man, and I know you didn't do anything that crazy Jasper said."

He suddenly felt even worse about the whole mess, and then it quickly turned to anger. The tea kettle in Jasper's mind had finally built up enough pressure that it just blew. "This is Jasper's fault," he yelled. At this point, everyone in the store was looking at him, but he was too mad to check himself. "He's a bully. Always thinking he has the upper hand. He made me so mad. One of these days he's going to pick on the wrong person and they're going to make him pay. It might even be me." Jasper surprised himself and the sisters with his outburst. He usually didn't say much, and he hardly ever showed any emotion. Realizing that all eyes were on him, he rushed out of the store. Rose ran after him, wanting to soothe him, but he had already got in the truck and sped off.

Daisy and Lily joined Rose at the door.

"Well, what do ya think about that?" Daisy said. Rose reached up and wiped away a tear that had rolled down her cheek.

Never had to pass the Cut Above; it was right on the main drag. As he passed it, he scowled. He drove on and was passing the Inn when he saw Billie in the front yard wrestling with some full garbage bags. He pulled in.

Momma and Pops had returned to the city. Georgie stayed a few more days. We had gone through a lot of the rooms and bagged up a lot of old ripped linens and broken dishes and such that Aunt Mae had collected through the years. She never threw anything out, thinking it would have a purpose later. It kept us busy and put our minds on something other than Uncle James. I was dragging one of the heavier bags out to Georgie's car when I heard someone pull into the driveway. I turned around, and it was Never in his old beat-up truck. It was spewing smoke like crazy. Never got out of the truck and ran up to me and took the heavy bags.

"Let me do that for you, Billie." Before I could say anything, he took it out of my hands. "Is this trash or something you want to keep?"

"Thanks, Jake. It is trash that I was going to take to the dump. There isn't room in my little bug for all of it, so I was putting it in Georgie's SUV."

"Oh, is Georgie here too? Oh, of course she is. I was really sorry to hear about James." Never started carrying the bag to his truck and threw it in the truck bed. He then started pulling the other bags out of the back of Georgie's SUV. "I'll just take these to the dump for you."

"Thank you, Jake."

"You can call me Never like everyone else. I'm kinda used to it. Only Mae calls me Jake." Georgie appeared at the door also dragging a bag. Never ran up and took the bag from her and put it in his truck.

In my peripheral, I could see movement from across the street at the Bait Shop. I turned and saw a young white lady with black hair whom I didn't know come out of the store and start walking toward us. I watched her as she neared where we were gathered by Never's truck.

"Hi, my name is Suzy Smith. I work across the road at the Bait Shop. I was wondering if you had a need for a part-time housekeeper. I could come over after I finish my shift at the Bait Shop. I'm a good worker. You can ask Mrs. Baits." She looked around as if to see who may be in charge. Her eyes rested for a while on Never. I watched her study him before she looked back at me when I spoke.

"If Mrs. Baits will vouch for you, that says a lot. I may take you up on your offer. I will have to think about it and get back to you."

"Okay, you can find me across the street or in the little cottage behind the store. Mrs. Baits is letting me stay there." She turned and walked back over to the Bait Shop.

"Got anything else?" Never asked.

"Not at the moment, but we are still cleaning. Having Suzy come over about a job gave me an idea. With Uncle James out of the picture for a while, and I don't know what Aunt Mae will need to do to take care of him once he is out of the hospital, we will need help with the stuff Uncle James took care of. If you could maybe come by and help with some of the chores around here, I'm sure we could work something out." I saw him hesitate. "It would be helping Uncle James and Aunt Mae."

"Oh, that is such a good idea, Billie. Never, you would be perfect. What do you think?" Never looked from Georgie to me. I could see the gears moving around in his mind.

"I guess I could do that."

"Perfect. I will clear it with Aunt Mae, and if you come by tomorrow about this time, it would be great," I said and held out my hand to shake with him. He wiped his hand off on his pants and reached out and took mine. Not wanting to be left out, Georgie put hers over top of ours and we all shook. Never got into his truck and went off in the direction of the dump. I looked across the street at the Bait Shop and could see Suzy standing in the door watching Never's truck go down the road. She saw me looking her way and disappeared into the store.

CHAPTER 14

When Aunt Mae makes up her mind, she acts on it right away. She spent most of her days (and some of her nights) at the hospital and left the running of the Inn to me. We didn't have any bookings, so the Inn was empty except for me and Georgie. Aunt Mae spent most of her time at the hospital. She didn't like the long drive back and forth, so she stayed with a friend who lived near the hospital. Georgie stayed and helped me clean for about a week but then started missing her babies, and I'm sure Marcus was tired of being a single father. So off she went, leaving me all alone in my Inn. All alone. All by myself. *I loved it.* I put on my socks and slid across the floors. I went back to binge-watching *Fresh Prince,* and even though I did think of Pig Slop now and then, I enjoyed my new life. Momma called me from time to time just to chat and probably see if I was okay by myself. She must have heard it in my voice that I was really okay.

Never came every day as promised and did any kind of odd jobs that I needed help with. The wood pile was always full. He even helped me finish painting a couple of the rooms. With a new color of a fresh coat of paint, the rooms looked so good I decided to paint them all with Never's help. About every other day I would go to the hospital and sit with Uncle James while Aunt Mae would get a rest. He was really looking a lot better and wasn't asking for a cigar as often.

"I'm so proud of you, Billie."

"Thank you, Uncle James. Why didn't you and Aunt Mae tell us you needed help with the Inn? I would have come sooner."

"We thought we were doing okay. We knew we weren't keeping it up as we would like, but this old Inn is all the world we knew. Plus, we felt we owed it to the founders of this beautiful resort to preserve our heritage.

You would have been amazed at how different it was during segregation." He reached for my hand, and his covered mine completely. He looked deep into my eyes as he recalled memories of what I can only imagine. "Almost everyone here was black, and we loved our village. We all had thriving businesses, and we didn't have to worry about stepping over the color barrier. We were safe here, and we all watched out for each other. It was different outside of the Village. As time went on, we saw completely black neighborhoods in the cities get demolished to make way for highways so that the white neighborhoods and businesses could be spared. Businesses that had been in people's families for generations, just like the white people's. It was passed down until more room had to be made for progress. Our history was nicely put as collateral damage except it was always at our expense. Our people's history was systematically being destroyed. We couldn't let that happen here. Now, because it is more integrated, it will probably stand the test of time. Don't get me wrong. Segregation was pure evil. We were all created by the same maker who, in his or her infinite wisdom, made us different on the outside but underneath still the same. Like the birds and the flowers and all living things that share this planet. Sorry, I guess I've had some time to really think about things." His gaze left mine to travel outside the window that was next to his bed.

"But we would have come. We would have . . ." He turned back to me and gave me an all-knowing look. The rest of the sentence didn't feel right to say at that moment. I really didn't know if my parents, who loved to teach, would have pulled up roots to run this Inn. Georgie and I couldn't do it as kids, but as adults, I think I would have been the only one who would have done it. In fact, I'm sure of it. Since I've been here, I can't imagine what took me so long to figure it out. Boy, am I slow.

"You all had your lives in the city. We didn't feel it would be fair. I guess we thought we could do this forever, but looking back, we just got too old. That too is God's plan."

"Uncle James, don't you worry about the Inn."

"I don't worry about it now. I know it's in good hands." He patted my hand as he said it.

"Ahem." Aunt Mae was standing in the doorway. I wondered how long she had been standing there until she spoke. "Don't let your uncle fool you. We knew you would eventually come, but we wanted you to come on your own. We often talked about it and wondered when. We were that sure, but when you didn't, we decided to give you a bit of a push. We saw it in your face every time you were here and how you seemed sad to leave. With your mother and father and even Georgie, it wasn't the same as it was for you. Yes, we knew you would come. We just thought it would be sooner."

"I guess we have that lowdown dog to thank for it," said Uncle James.

"James, you need to adjust your filter." Uncle James looked like he got caught with one of his cigars. "Don't listen to him, Billie. It's the drugs that make him talk too much." She shook her head. I actually laughed, and they both joined me.

The morning light was coming earlier and earlier. With no one in the Inn, I could have stayed in bed a bit longer. I had some sulking to catch up on, but instead, I got up early the next morning and fixed myself an elaborate morning meal of a frozen breakfast burrito and coffee. A cook I am not, but I could heat up a mean breakfast burrito. It wasn't much, but it was enough fuel to put me to work.

I had been working so hard cleaning and moving some things around and making things more my style. I kept the Amazon truck busy with many deliveries so after I pulled in all the things they had just dropped off, I decided I really needed to work on the attic if I was going to start letting guests stay up there. Uncle James and Aunt Mae hardly ever let anyone stay up there. It was so big and a lot of work if a family used the space, so it was hardly ever used unless it was us. But I was going to change that. Yup. There was a new sheriff in town. I motioned with my fingers like I was shooting guns with each hand, blew on one of them, gave them a twirl before I holstered my imaginary guns. I gave my imaginary cowgirl hat a tap and winked at no one. This is what happens when you have a lot of alone time and an active imagination.

At that moment, my stomach started growling. I looked at my watch, and wow, it was dinnertime. Maybe I would pop down to one of the restaurants or over to the Water's Edge for something to eat. But you know how you start in one direction and find yourself doing something else? Instead of going for something to eat, I headed upstairs to the attic. I took the keychain that Uncle James gave me and stood in front of Private. I knew someday I was going to have to face my fear of a closet. As ridiculous as that sounds, it was very real to me. I stood in front of Private as I had when I was six except I had on shoes this time. I blew air out of my clenched lips and stuck the key in the lock and gave it a turn. I slowly opened the door.

"Aaaaaaaaah," I screamed and jumped as a ragtop mop fell out. I looked in Private and breathed a sigh of relief. Ha ha, no boogeyman. I felt good and ridiculous at the same time.

My mind wandered back to that no-good Pig Slop. I started singing an Aretha Franklin tune. "R-E-S-P-E-C-T. That's not what you gave to me," I paraphrased, thinking of Pig Slop. I reached for a bottle of Pine-Sol and opened it. I set the open bottle on the shelf. One by one I took out the broom, some rags, the bucket, and picked up the mop. I dropped all on the floor but the mop. Still in my Aretha Franklin frame of mind, I started dancing and using the mop handle as my mic, still singing my version of "Respect." "P-I-G-S-L-O-P, that is what you are to me." Then not able to make up more stuff to sing that caught the real slime of a lowlife that Pig Slop was, I started humming.

Still humming and dancing to the tune, I filled the bucket with hot water and went back to get the bottle of Pine-Sol cleaner. I reached in, and just as I grabbed the Pine-Sol, there stood the old man who had not been there just seconds before.

"Aaaaaaaaah!" we both shrieked, and I dropped the Pine-Sol. As it dropped, it splashed all over me. I started backpedaling and tripped over the bucket, knocking it over. Water went all over the floor, and then the bucket took a trip down the stairs. Lucky for me I had on shoes this time, so I didn't run through the door. I looked again, yep, he was still there. "Aaaaaaaaah!" I started screaming again and followed the bucket down the steps until I passed it and ran right out of the Inn.

I kept running until I reached the Water's Edge. From outside, I could hear Marvin Gaye singing "What's Going On!" I was wondering the same thing, Marvin. What the heck is going on? I ran through the door not making eye contact with anyone. I kept going until I got to the bar and hiked up on a vacant bar stool. Today Tony was in his usual spot behind the bar, talking to some customers. He saw me run in and excused himself. He walked down to where I had just plopped myself down, my heart still racing.

"Hi, Billie. How are things at the Inn? Uncle James okay?"

He looked at my face and analyzed it like a doctor. Without a word, he poured me a Jack Daniel's on the rocks. Being a good bartender, he waited patiently for me to spill whatever brought me in so quickly. He watched in silence as I downed my drink. I'm sure he noticed my hand that held my glass was shaking, but he didn't say a word. I didn't know what to say because every time I thought of what to say, it sounded crazy. "Well, in case you didn't know it, I have a ghost in my Inn." "Funny thing, there is a ghost in my Private closet." "Has anyone ever seen ghosts at the Inn? I have." "Have you ever had one of those days when a ghost appears?" I settled for "Uncle James is doing better. I just really needed a drink and wanted to get here before you closed."

"Good thing you got here when you did, Billie. You just made it with only three hours to spare."

I blew some air through my clenched lips. "I guess I have been working a bit hard getting the Inn ready to be reopened and lost track of time."

Tony smiled. "I guess that is why you ran in here like Florence Griffith-Joyner and without a coat." He slowly bent toward me and, with his lips real close to my ear said, "By the way, I love your new high-end perfume, Lysol by Versace, but aren't you putting it on a little thick?" He moved back to his stance.

"It's Pine-Sol for your information. I spilled it. Would you stop working on your comedy act and go back to being a bartender and fix me another Jack?" I held up my empty glass and gave it a shake.

I saw him try not to smile, but it was too late. It had reached his eyes. He poured me another one and slid it in front of me. I picked up the drink and quickly drank it down. All of it. About then, Tory, one of the waitresses, had walked up and had a drink order that she needed filled. She told Tony what she needed and then turned to me.

"Hi, Billie. Glad you decided to run the Inn. Your aunt and uncle have been struggling with it for some time now. Heard about Uncle James. Hope he is doing better. Do you know you smell terrible, like cleaning solution?" Tony snickered at that comment and then excused himself and went about filling the drink orders.

"Hi, Tory. I kinda spilled Pine-Sol on my clothes. Uncle James is fine, thanks for asking."

Tory always said what she thought. The girl had no filter. "Girl, you should have changed before coming in here. I would have. I know you probably brought limited clothes since I doubt much would fit in that little car of yours, so if you want to borrow something of mine, just let me know." She was probably trying to be nice. Since I looked like I was standing in a deep hole when I was next to her, there is no way any of her clothes wouldn't look ridiculous on me.

"Thanks, Tory. I may take you up on that." Never.

"Was that guy you were going to marry really married already? I showed Tony and John your YouTube. What a—"

"Here's the drink order, Tory," Tony, overhearing some of the conversation while fixing the drinks, suddenly interrupted before she could finish. "I think your table is signaling that they want their drinks."

"Yeah, whatever." And then, remembering who signs her paychecks, she finished with a dazzling smile. Or was it something else? I still didn't know who the mystery girl was, but considering the recent development at the Inn, it took a backseat in my "worry" lineup. "Thanks, Tony. I'll talk to you later, Billie." She walked off, balancing the drink order over her shoulder on the tray.

"Bye bye." I waved my fingers cheerfully after her. I can hardly wait for our talk.

Tony looked at me for a moment and said, "You're not drinking because of your ex-fiancé are you, Billie? He wasn't good enough for you, you know. Last summer, when you paraded him around here—"

"Paraded him around?" I interrupted very indignantly.

"Yes, and he acted like he was too good for this place. Turning up his nose to everything. Checking out the girls at the beach through those stupid sunglasses when you weren't looking. I knew you would never be happy with him. I would have liked to have broken his nose too." Geesh, just how much did everyone know about what happened with Pig Slop? And how did they . . . Georgie and her big mouth.

"Look, would you just pour me another one and get out of my business?" To tell the truth, I was glad that he wanted to break Pig Slop's nose. I was also glad that he thought that was the reason I was getting sloshed so that I didn't have to come up with one. I don't think there is ever a good segway into telling someone about a ghost in your home. That made me wonder if anyone else ever had this happen to them. But at the same time, I still didn't know what to do. Tony poured me another one and slipped away while I sat there reevaluating reality.

CHAPTER 15

I sat there thinking that I must be losing my mind or whether I inhaled too much Pine-Sol. I just saw the same old man in the same old-fashioned clothes whom I thought I saw when I was a kid. And then he disappeared, so I'm pretty sure he's a ghost. If I tell anybody, it will be like I was six again. People will look at me like I'm "touched in the head." Yup. I can still remember when I came to after fainting. I was still on the floor but surrounded by everyone in the Inn. Momma had me draped in her arms, Pops was touching the big bump on my head, even Georgie looked worried. Uncle James had put a blanket over me while Aunt Mae had a wet washcloth that she kept moving across my face, attempting to cool me down. The hotel guest had all gathered around too. I could hear the concern for me in their whispering voices. Who I didn't see was the old man in Private and wondered where he had vanished to.

"Where's the old man, Momma?" I wanted to know.

"What old man, honey?" Momma asked.

"The old man in Private." I asked. I saw my family exchanging looks with each other.

"We call the closet 'Private,'" Georgie explained.

Almost simultaneously they all denied any old man was there.

"Sweetie, you bumped your head when you fell," Pops tried to reason with me.

"It's a closet and it is always locked. We keep our cleaning supplies in it just like the one we have on the main floor," said Uncle James.

My parents at this moment were trying very hard to keep me quiet, worried that I may have had a concussion or lost my mind. I started whining and crying that I saw him. Uncle James pulled a long keychain he always wore out of his pocket with keys to all the doors on it. He quickly walked over to Private and opened it. I strained to see beyond everyone in its path until they all slowly moved out of the way. I could see that it was a shallow closet and all that was in there was some cleaning supplies, buckets, mops, and brooms. There was no man in it, nor was there any room for one to be in it.

"There, there, sweetie. It is only a closet. There is no man. You bumped your head very hard," said Momma. By this time, the village doctor had arrived. He was a very kind-looking light-brown man with a lot of freckles. His name was Dr. Simpson. He examined my bump thoroughly and did some coordination checks before saying, "She has a nasty bump, but it doesn't appear to be anything you need to worry about." Then he smiled and said to me, "You will be up and playing soon."

He was right. After the mandatory bed rest that Momma put me on, I was up and playing, swimming, and having a great time. I almost forgot about the old man in Private. Well, I could have if everyone hadn't teased me about it. Even back then, Georgie had a big mouth and told everyone that I saw Casper in the closet. That jerk Pudgy was relentless. John and Tony were the only kids who didn't tease me about it. I found out a few years ago from John that Aunt Birdie threatened their lives if they said one thing to me about it. The adults thought I had an overactive imagination, and I must have made him up. It did seem like a bad dream. And I made sure that I didn't go by Private; in fact, I did my best to avoid it. Whenever I had to walk past it, I didn't. I ran.

"Billie, stop that running. You might fall again," yelled Momma.

By the time we were packed up to go home at the end of our stay, I was starting to think they were right. I must have made him up in my childish mind. As we got in the car and started to pull away, I looked out of the back window and up at the attic window. I saw the little man wave to me as we drove out of the driveway onto the road. That's when I started screaming again.

So do I really want to go through all of that again? I think not. I can just see the whole conversation playing out before me if I called Chief Pudgy Harris. Yup, our bully was now chief of police. As you can guess, he was a good eater, and although his real name was Lewis, Pudgy stuck through adulthood. Pudgy had been relentless when I saw the ghost the first time. He made fun of me every summer after that incident. I think as an adult with authority, he wouldn't be any better. And I don't think that exorcism is one of the things he received in his police training. I looked around the bar to see if there was anyone that I could possibly tell when I noticed that everyone in the bar looked a bit blurred. Tony chose this time to return his attention to me.

"I just want you to know that if or when you are ready to talk, I am here." His face came in and out of focus, but it was really a nice face. I wonder why I hadn't noticed that before. I had known Tony all my life and never once thought of him being anything more than my buddy next door. The third drink had had a calming effect, and now I stopped thinking so hard about the old man in Private and more about the young one standing in front of me.

"I'm not upset. I just got tired of cleaning."

"Okay, Billie. I know your aunt and uncle are away, and if you need any help, just ask. You don't have to go it alone, you know."

"Look, jush pour annuder one." I guess only having a breakfast burrito this morning was not enough to absorb the Jack Daniel triplets. It didn't get past Tony's trained bartender's eye that I was becoming a bit sloshed, so he watered down the next one when he thought I wasn't looking.

"Here ya go!" he said as he placed it in front of me. It wasn't even the right color, but I didn't say anything. It was free after all.

Tony moved down the bar to a couple of new customers who had slid up to the bar. I sat there letting the Jack burn up what was left of my brain cells. The room took on a bit of a spin, and my stomach was feeling funny, and I don't mean ha-ha either. Before I could help it, I started to smile that lazy smile that drunk people get like they know a secret but don't. After fixing drinks and taking food orders for the other customers, Tony walked back up to where I was sitting. He started wiping out clean glasses from the little sink behind the bar.

"Would you like something to eat, Billie? Or maybe a pot of coffee?" Tony said as he put down the towel. He saw me sway a little. He quickly lifted the little bar gate and walked around to where I was sitting. He cupped my face in his hands. He was looking to see how dilated my pupils were. In my liquored-up state, I totally misread that.

"You know, if I didn't hate men sho mush, I might think you are kinna cute." Who the heck said that? I was actually flirting with Tony. And then I puckered up my lips for the kiss that didn't come and puked breakfast burrito on both me and Tony. The only good thing that happened after that was I passed out, so I didn't have to see any of the faces from my walk of shame through the bar. Well, it wasn't a walk; I was told later by Tory that Tony caught me before I fell off the bar stool and carried me to his living quarters off the bar where I slept it off.

CHAPTER 16

When I finally woke up, it was late morning. I tried to pry my eyes open, but the light in the room was relentless. I lay there a while, and then things slowly started returning to my memory. Geesh! I sure am putting my life back together. Let's see, I got humiliated, got fired, got arrested, got a ghost, and then got humiliated again. And I smell like puke and Pine-Sol. Geesh! I lay there thinking, *How bad do I smell?* Could I stand it until someone else gives me something to wear, or is it bad enough that I am going to have to go back to the Inn and hope not to see Casper? I got up, and although my head felt like I slept on a pillowcase full of rocks, I felt okay. There was a beautiful crocheted afghan and a pillow on the floor.

I snatched off the stinky burrito-, Pine-Sol-, puke-smelling shirt I had on and looked for a trash can. Found it and threw my shirt in it. I took a sniff, and my bra didn't smell as bad, so I kept it on. I could still smell puke and figured out it must be in my hair. I looked around the room for one of Tony's shirts. I found a T-shirt laying on top of a wingback chair that said "I'm Too Sexy For This Shirt" and picked it up and tossed it on the bed. Oh brother, I can't believe Tony would have a shirt like this. But beggars can't be choosers. I bent down and picked my shoes up off the floor. Ow and ewww. That did hurt my head, and I got another whiff of my stinky hair. When I stood up, I really got a good look at Tony's room. When the boys took over the Water's Edge from their parents, Tony converted one of the offices into his bedroom. He said it was because he wanted people to know someone was always there on guard, not that anyone had ever attempted to break in. Most of us don't feel the need to lock the doors at night. I'm sure it was because he wasn't ready to have his own place but still could have some privacy. I saw this room after he had converted it, but he made some nice improvements since, and he kept it neat. John had a small cottage around the lake.

It was a typical man's room (I guess I wouldn't know because I had a typical girl's room at home). Something caught my eye and made me go over and take a closer look. No, it wasn't a whip or cat-o-nines or a maid's black-and-white uniform. On a bookshelf was Tony's collection of little die-cast cars, buses, and trucks all sitting on top of little yellow boxes with matching pictures of the toy. Lots of them, all different colors and styles. Some were in sets. I picked up a little car and really looked at it. On the bottom it said Dinky Toys. I remember how he collected them as a kid and smiled. His grandfather had started the collection and gave it to Tony when he was a boy. It looked like Tony still collected them and was still a kid at heart.

About then I heard Tony's voice in the hall getting closer to the bedroom door, talking to someone in the bar no doubt. Maybe about me. I couldn't face him now. I rolled my eyes and blew out air and did what I thought was best. I made a grab for his "Sexy" shirt off the bed, opened the window, and climbed out. OMG it was cold, and the sunlight pierced my head. I shaded my eyes against it. Lucky for me, Tony's room was on the first floor, but unlucky for me that John was sitting on a deck chair nearby smiling at me.

"Good morning, Billie." He said it like this happened a lot. He had a cigarette in his hand and took a drag. There was also a cup on the table next to him. It probably held coffee with a little Baileys mixed in.

"Um, hi, John. How's it going?" I waved Tony's shirt at him. Tony picked this time to poke his head out of his window.

"You may want to put that on," Tony said, grinning from ear to ear. Geesh! What was wrong with me. I quickly pulled it over my head and scrambled off. I heard him yell, "See ya!" Yes, you did, didn't you? It was really looking a lot better to face the ghost after this humiliation.

I got to the kitchen door and slowly opened it. I peeked in but didn't see Casper. I didn't know if I was shivering because I didn't have on a coat or because I was scared or both. Okay, it was both, but mostly scared. I took a deep breath and went through the door. I left it open a crack and then changed my mind and left it wide open in case I had to make another quick exit. I turned on every light switch I passed even though it was morning and light. I grabbed a sweater off the back of a chair and pulled it around me. I wanted to shower and wash my hair but was afraid Casper would float in and say "Boo," so I just stood by the front stairway and looked up. I waited for a while, not knowing what to do. I thought about just jumping in my bug and going back home. But then I looked around me at the Inn and decided I wasn't going to let anyone or anything take this away from me. I blew out air and got my courage up.

"Ok-k-kay C-C-Casper, I know y-y-you are up there, c-c-come on out n-n-now," I yelled into thin air. My knees were shaking so bad I was barely able to stand. It probably sounded more like I was riding over all those ruts in the road in Pops's Pontiac because I was shaking so bad. "I know you're h-h-here." I waited a minute. Ha, maybe I scared my ghost away. I stood straighter and yelled, "C-C-Casper! You better come d-d-down here." And then I pulled a Momma. *"You come down here now!"* I said more forcefully than what I felt. I even did the side-to-side snake-head motion and pointed my finger downward. If he had shown up, I would have probably peed right there on the floor.

The silence was killing me. Not knowing what to do next, I shook my head and walked to the common room and plopped down on the sofa. The adrenaline that I had, left. I was spent. The only thing keeping me grounded was the smell of puke in my hair. I sat there until the silence just about drove me crazy. I was about to reach for the remote just to have some sound when I looked up on the floor lamp next to me, and there was Casper.

Totally out of my element, I raised my hand in a small wave, did a nervous laugh, and said, "H-h-hi."

My ectoplasmic visitor said, "Hi."

"Aaaaaaaah!" I screamed, and so did he. I jumped up and ran into my room and shut the door. I tried to pull myself together and opened the door. I peeked into the common room, and yep, he was still there sitting on the lamp. I slowly walked in and sat down on the sofa. Neither of us said anything for what seemed a while until I couldn't stand it any longer. "Why didn't you come out when I first yelled at you?" I asked. It felt funny (not of the ha-ha kind either) to be chastising a ghost.

"You called someone named Caster. I wasn't sure if Caster was going to show up. Or if you were a bit touched in the head because no one else was here," he replied. "I don't know nobody named Caster."

"Geesh! It's Cas-*per.*" I took a deep breath and tried to make this ridiculous situation sane. "What is your name?"

"Ezekiel Bradford, but most called me Zeke." He had been dead for some time by the style of his clothes.

"Okay, Zeke. I'm Billie. Can you just leave? I own this place, and I really can't have a ghost living here. Sorry, um, staying here." This was impossible.

"I don't have anywhere else to go. This here's my home. Always has been since Jackson Bradford gave it to me."

"Oh so you are . . . were the caretaker." I looked up at him again. Not only do I have a ghost, but he's also an old ghost. "Could you come down from there so that I don't get a stiff neck?" I watched him slowly float down until he was sitting on the sofa right next to me. It freaked me out a bit. "I-I-I changed my mind. You can g-g-go back up there." I stuttered and pointed at the top of the lamp. He floated back up to his perch.

"You don't understand. I can't have a g . . . you . . . liv . . . staying here. This is an Inn. I have guests or will have guests. I can't have you scaring them or me."

"Why would I scare somebody? I never hurt nobody in my life. I never meant to scare you either. I just never had nobody who could see me before." He paused for a moment and then said, "I'm really sorry that I scared you when you were a little girl, but to be fair, you scared me too."

"You never had anyone see you before?" Just my luck. I was feeling less afraid at this point and more annoyed—no, not annoyed, curious. Zeke was starting to feel, well, a little less spooky. "Why can I see you?"

"I don't know. I don't write the rules." Good point. Since we had both calmed down a lot and I still smelled terrible, I felt that I could reason with Zeke. "Look, I think we both need some time to think about this situation, and I really need to get cleaned up. Can you go back to Private and stay there until I call you?"

"Private?"

"The closet in the attic. I'm guessing that closet is your home or something."

"It's not a closet."

"I know. It's your home, I guess."

"I mean it's not a closet. It just looks like one."

"What do you mean it's not a closet?"

"I'll show you." I guess my shower was going to wait. I followed him as he floated up two flights of stairs. I was still turning all the lights on.

I don't know how that helps when you are dealing with a ghost, but I did it just the same.

We were standing in front of Private. Well, I was, but Zeke was floating in front of it.

"Is there any way that you could just walk and not float? It's still a bit unnerving for me. I may have had a breakdown in the past few hours, so I would prefer things be as normal for me as possible." Zeke looked at me with concern and floated down until he was standing on the floor next to me. I fought the urge to run. I then looked around. Private was still standing open as it had when I left in a hurry, but the water from the bucket and the Pine-Sol that had spilled all over the floor was gone. Everything had been neatly put away.

"Did you clean all this up?" He nodded. Hmm. There may be an advantage to having a ghost in the Inn. Then he walked into Private and disappeared through the back of the closet. Okay, that was scary, and I got that urge to run again. I didn't, but I thought about it. After a few minutes went by and no Zeke, I said, "Ah, hello. I'm not sure what you want to show me, but I can't walk through walls."

Zeke poked his head out of the back of the closet, just his head. "Oh, sorry. This is kind of new to me. This is stuck. Haven't used it in years. Do you have any tools?"

CHAPTER 17

Jasper was still fuming over the incident with Never. What was worse, that busybody Baits woman came in right after he slapped Rachel. He held himself back when she came in and started fussing all over Rachel. And Rachel. Always the victim. The nerve of her to question his actions. He saw what he saw, and that was Never putting his filthy hands on her. No telling what the trash would have done if he hadn't shown up. Not that he cared about Rachel, but she was his property, and no one was going to make him the laughingstock of the town. If he didn't learn anything from his worthless father, he did learn that his wife was his property and will not ever make him look bad to others.

When Jasper was a child, his mother left his father and took him to Michigan to live with some of her relatives. They were there for a few months, and Jasper was starting to feel safe and happy. He even made some friends, something he didn't have back at home. People avoided their family, especially Frank, who had a short fuse and was subject to go off for the slightest reason. But here in Michigan, his relatives showed love and affection. They would often bring him to the Enchanted Village to the Big Dipper for ice cream, something else he had never had. He remembered wondering why so many black people were around. Oh, he saw a lot of them in Mississippi, but here they owned everything, and there was pride. It was different.

But then his father found them and brought them back to Mississippi. He beat his mother so bad she never tried to leave again. He told her he would kill her if she ever thought about it. Jasper never forgave his mother for coming back to this life. He didn't understand her peril. He had witnessed her beatings all his life, so he didn't think it was a big deal. No, he held it against her for the rest of his life instead of putting the blame where it belonged—on the abuser. He became an abuser himself.

If that Baits woman hadn't come in when she did, he would have made Rachel sorry for trying to protect that trash. Although he was doing well with his butcher shop, he was done with it. He never really wanted it in the first place, but he had inherited it from one of his mother's uncles, who had a stipulation that he had to run it for 10 years before he could sell it or it would go to another relative. Five years felt like a lifetime to him. And then Rachel's mother messed up a lot of Jasper's plans by threatening to put him in jail for rape if he didn't marry Rachel. Rachel! That sorry piece of meat.

He thought back some years ago when he first saw her. He had gone to Louisville to see a woman about some used butcher equipment that her recently deceased husband owned. Her name was Ida, and her husband had died unexpectedly. She was practically giving it away. She had an old barn behind the house where her husband kept all his stuff that he bought in auctions. They were haggling over the price when her daughter, Rachel, came home from high school. Jasper liked them young, and when the old lady wasn't looking, he winked at Rachel.

He decided to extend his stay in Louisville. The next day, he waited for her at her school and offered her a ride. He took her to a nice restaurant, and she was so trusting she thought he was really something and instantly fell for his lies. But after he got what he wanted, he went back to the Village. Three months later, Jasper got a phone call from Ida. Rachel was pregnant, and if he didn't marry her, she was going to call the authorities. He went down to Louisville, married her at the courthouse, and brought her back to the Village. He abused her both physically and mentally until she lost the baby. Then he blamed her for losing his baby, and that brought on even more abuse. But he liked owning something he had power over, just like his father.

But now since his father died, he wanted her out. He had plans now that he found out Rachel recently received a big, fat inheritance check. To think that she thought she hid it from him. But he found it by accident, and now he had all of it under the till in the register.

But now he wondered how he got in the predicament. He was tired of the butcher shop, Rachel, and this life. The good thing was that he had the money, and Rachel was going to go back to Louisville. Hopefully for good, but that could also be a problem. He didn't want her to get any of his money; yeah, he felt he earned it. He wasn't sure how divorce worked. The few friends he had who were divorced all complained about their ex-wives taking them for everything they had. Nope, she is not getting her hands on his money. And then there was Never. But wait a minute. Maybe some good can come out of this. He had a plan.

All week after that incident Rachel was packing up all the things that she had that she didn't want to part with. She had no plans of ever coming back. Forget that madness. She would get a lawyer to get her inheritance money back from Jasper. He thought he was so smart. He didn't know she found his extra cell phone. She knew better than to confront him with it and well, she really didn't care.

On the day she was leaving, she filled up her small car with most of her things. She didn't know where Jasper was. She would rather not see him again. All she wanted to do was to get away. That thing with Never was the last straw. She drove out on the main road and stopped at the Save N Stop gas station. She was filling her tank when she remembered her locket in the register. It had a photograph of her and her father in it, and she couldn't bear to leave it behind. She finished filling her tank and then headed back to the Cut Above. It was Sunday, and the butcher shop was closed. The streets were pretty vacant. She pulled in and got out her key and opened the door. The little bell tinkled. She walked over to the register and heard a noise too late behind her and then blackness.

CHAPTER 18

I ran downstairs to get the toolbox taking the steps two at a time. When I got down to the last step in full run mode, I turned and ran right into Tony (yes, another scream), who caught me before I fell. I backed up out of his arms.

"What are you doing here, and how did you get in?" I guess I should have been glad that I ran into a living person, but I was starting to get used to the idea of Zeke.

"You left the backdoor wide open. Is this going to be a thing with you, Billie?" He stood there staring at me as he stuffed his hands in his pockets.

"What are you talking about?"

"Running everywhere and"—he leaned into me and took a sniff—"smelling bad." I backed up.

"Are you here for a reason? I have stuff to do."

"I just came to check on you. You seem, I don't know, a bit on the crazy side." Crazy—boy, I could tell him about crazy. "You get drunk and puke on me. I just wanted to make sure you are okay."

"Technically you got me drunk, and now I'm not so sure it wasn't a bad breakfast burrito." Before he could say anything about that, I held up my finger. "Sorry I puked on you. I guess it was my fault. But I'm fine. I'll come over and wash your linens. They probably smell bad." He smiled.

"I already washed my sheets. I found your T-shirt in the trash. I'm assuming you don't want it back." He raised his eyebrows.

"No. I don't."

"You going to tell me what's up and why you felt you had to go out of my bedroom window?"

I decided to get him off the subject by turning the tables on him.

"What about you, Mr. I'm Too Sexy for My Shirt? Who buys a shirt like this anyway?" I said pointing at the shirt. Ha! I felt like I got some of my own back. I didn't want to tell him about John's information about him dating, but it didn't keep me from fishing for it.

"I didn't buy it. It was given to me." Oh great. I'm wearing a present from his secret girlfriend. He reached around behind me and fished out a tag in the neck of it. "The tag is still on it. I wouldn't be caught dead in it. Glad you got some use of it." He was smiling, and I knew he was making fun of me. That burned me up, or was it the shirt or the girlfriend? I don't know, but I was getting mad, and besides, I couldn't keep a ghost waiting forever, could I? I guess that is kind of a dumb question once you think about it.

"And you're not all that sexy either." Who was I kidding? He was all that and more. He reached up and raked his hands through his hair.

"I didn't come over here to fight with you about a shirt. I just wanted to make sure that after your visit at the bar last night and your exit"—he broke into smile—"out of my bedroom window this morning that you were all right." I was getting ticked off. Plus I could see Zeke peeking down from the ceiling. Just his head. Tony saw me looking at the ceiling and looked up to see what I was looking at. Seeing nothing, he looked back at me.

"Get out, Tony. I'm fine. I was just getting ready to shower and stuff when you came in. Is there anything else?" I was pushing him in the direction of the door. I really didn't want an answer, and I really didn't like the one he gave.

"Yeah, John wants to know when the next show starts." He was laughing now. Blowing out air, I pushed him out of the door and locked it. I rested against the closed door for a moment. I could hear Tony laughing as he walked away. I looked up to where Zeke's head had been, but it wasn't there now. I went to find the tools.

I found the toolbox not knowing what else my new friend may need. I dragged the heavy box up two flights of stairs. Not seeing Zeke, I yelled for him, "Hey, Zeke, I'm back." He materialized next to me so unexpectedly that I dropped it. It hit the floor with a bang. We both jumped. "Hey, we really need to have some rules around here. I am still trying to get used to you, and I'm pretty sure you are doing the same with me. Would you just not . . . that?" I said, waving my hands at him. Zeke nodded his head and looked in the toolbox. He pulled out a screwdriver and went back into Private. He was careful to show me what he was doing. He took the screwdriver and pried open a piece of intricately carved molding. Instead of falling off, it flipped up, revealing a catch of some kind. I closed it and ran my fingers over it. Unless you knew it was there, you couldn't see it. Zeke flipped it back open.

"He seems like a nice guy," he casually said. I blew out air.

"Who seems like a nice guy?" Like I didn't know who he was talking about.

"Your gentleman caller. I heard all that commotion and decided I better see if you were okay. Why were you arguing with him?"

"Look, I don't want to talk about it." Since most of this ridiculous episode was because of Zeke. "What are you showing me?"

"He was really concerned about you." I guess he wasn't going to let it go.

"He is my friend from next door. Friend. Brother-like. What are you trying to show me?"

"The hinges need to be oiled. I wanted to show you how to open it or I would have just popped it open. This hasn't been opened since I . . ." He faltered for words. I suddenly felt deep sorrow for him. It had to be hard all these years doing whatever a ghost does. Before I could comment on it, he stuck his finger in, and I heard a click. The whole back of Private swung open. Zeke then broke out with a great big smile as if to say "See" and beckoned me in.

Okay, now this was spooky and the plot to all scary movies. I am not going to be like all the other stupid women who just went in and were chopped up or something.

"Ah, hey Z-Z-Z-Zeke, I really d-d-don't think I want t-t-to go in there. I really n-n-need to shower and read W-W-War and Peace and w-w-watch Roots, all of them, probably should shave m-m-my legs and . . ." I was beginning to rethink running the Loving Arms. Suddenly a vision of twin girls in blue dresses with pink ribbons standing in a hallway and a kid on a tricycle ran through my mind. "I don't think I c-c-can—"

Zeke interrupted me, "Please trust me, Billie. I wouldn't let anything happen to you." With that, he walked through the back of Private. I sighed, bit my bottom lip, and picked up a flashlight out of the toolbox. I took a deep breath, turned the flashlight on, and, timidly and against better judgment, followed him in. I bounced my light all around. "Are there m-m-more . . . people . . . like you in here Z-Z-Zeke?" I asked through chattering teeth. "Z-Z-Zeke?" I didn't hear or see him. "Zeke, if you j-j-j-jump out and say 'b-b-boo,' I will prob-b-bably join you in the h-h-hereafter." Why did I say that? He may want me to join him. "Zeke?"

"Here I am. I went to get a lantern." I heard him strike a match and could now see him illuminated in the match's glow. Then he lit the old-fashioned lantern that he held in his hand. The room came to light but still very dim. As he swung the lantern around so that I could get a better look, I could see that it was the size of a very large bedroom. I walked around the room with Zeke holding the lantern keeping pace with me. It was filled with beautiful antique furniture and furnishings. There were all types of old-looking wooden toys. It didn't look like a bedroom but a play area where an adult, probably Mr. Bradford, could sit and watch his son or even play with him comfortably.

"Zeke, have you been living in this room all this time?"

"I have. When I first"—he struggled to say the word—"died."

"Passed over," I helped him.

"Yes, passed over, no one could see or hear me. I went all around the Village, and there was no one like me, and no one knew I was there. After that I never left the house. I thought that no one would ever see me. Was I ever surprised when a little girl saw me and screamed."

"Does my aunt and uncle know about this room?" I asked, still looking around it in awe.

"No. Unless you knew how to open the back, you can't get in. Here is the button to close it or open it from this side too." He showed me by pushing the button, and all of a sudden, the opening closed. The light in the lantern flickered but stayed lit. Good thing. I could see myself breaking a cartoon silhouette opening of myself through the back of the closet. I quickly reached up and opened it back up.

"Why do you want to stay here? You could probably go anywhere in the world." And then he said something that I totally understood.

"I love this old house. I can't imagine being any place else."

I looked at Zeke, and he was looking back at me. We both were trying to figure out where we go from here. It was then I made a decision. "Okay, if you promise not to come into my bedroom, I will respect your privacy here in Private and only come in if invited. That goes for my bathroom too." I don't know what kind of power I had over making a ghost keep his word, but Zeke nodded his head and I wanted to believe him.

"I agree." I was so relieved. And now I felt I could go and shower.

When I got out of the shower and changed my clothes, I felt so much better. I saw Tony's Sexy shirt laying on the bathroom floor where I threw it when I took it off and picked it up. I tore the tag off and put it in with a load of wash I had to do. Getting back to doing regular chores helped put back some normalcy. As I went down the steps to the basement to the washing machine I wondered if someday I'd find a dragon or troll or something down there. Geesh!

CHAPTER 19

That night was a fitful one. I listened for every sound in the Inn. I wasn't as brave as I felt when it was light outside. I didn't think Zeke was going to hurt me, but he is a ghost. I slept with the light on. The next morning, I got up and went into the office and momentarily looked around as I often did. I marveled at the craftsmanship of the builder and of course Mr. Bradford, who had designed every inch of the Inn. I loved to sit behind the beautiful old desk that had been the only piece of furniture recovered from the Bradford estate. That is, until finding the things inside Private. I walked around the desk and sat down in the large leather desk chair. It made a creaking noise as it accepted my weight. I touched the secret panel on the desk leg where Aunt Mae used to hide candy for me and Georgie. It popped out, and lo and behold, there was some candy that must have been put there many years ago and forgotten. I touched the secret button, and the panel closed. I shook my head as if lifting the cobwebs of yesterday and got busy looking over all the new bookings. Throughout the day, the phone rang off the hook with new reservations. This summer was going to be very busy.

"Ah, Billie?" I jumped and papers flew everywhere. Zeke was peeking in the doorway. "Sorry." He floated into the office and helped me pick them up. He handed me what he gathered and then went back into the hall and peeked in. "Is it okay if I come in?"

"Sure, Zeke. is there something on your mind?" I shuffled the papers into a neat stack and put them in a drawer. Zeke floated in and hovered in the air. I pointed to a chair, and he sat down.

"You never told me who you were yellin' for. That Caster fellow. Who is it?" He looked at me questioningly.

"Not Caster . . . Cas-*per*. Casper the friendly . . ." Oh boy. "Follow me." I got up and headed for the common room. Zeke took his seat on top of the lamp while I sat down on the sofa. I reached into the basket for the right remote and turned on the TV. Up to now, I guess Zeke had never seen a TV. He floated down and studied it from all angles. He even stuck his head through it. He tried to touch the things on the programs.

"Can they hear you?" He asked as he floated back from it and scratched his head.

"In this case I am like you. They can't hear or see me." He nodded his head thoughtfully and went over to inspect it some more.

"Umm hmm. How did you get the little people in the tray?" He looked behind it, under it, and all around it.

"They aren't little people. Well, I guess they kind of are but not real." Hmm. This was difficult. I picked up my cell and Googled "television." No help there either. Wikipedia explained it as "a telecommunication medium used for transmitting moving images in monochrome (black and white), or in color, and in two or three dimensions and sound." Nope, no help there. "It's called either a television or a TV. The things in it kind of float through the air like you do but end up in this . . . tray. Didn't you ever come in here at all in this century?"

"No. I told you, nobody could see me, so I just stayed in my room." I think he became less interested in how television worked and more in what was on the screen because he went back up on his perch. I flipped through some channels and watched his face. It went through many emotions. He was fascinated. He would comment from time to time about fast food, prescriptions, or insurance commercials. But he really lit up with one commercial.

"*What is that?*" He saw a Cadillac commercial with Regina King.

"It's called a car. That is how we all get around now."

"What? What? Are there still horses and wagons? Do you have one of those . . . cars?"

"There are still horses, not really any wagons except at some farms, and I have a car, but it doesn't look anything like that." I walked over to the side window and pointed at my bug. He kind of shimmed he was so excited. "People ride horses for fun now, and there are lots of cars on the roads. All different kinds and all different colors."

"How do you feed it?" I should have become a teacher like my parents. Then I would be more prepared for answers.

"They run on a liquid called gas. Don't ask me how because I don't know. There is a lot that you missed out on through the years that I can't explain. Just keep watching, and I will try." The commercial went off. I channel-surfed and he absorbed everything like a ghostly sponge. As we watched all the different shows, I noticed that he watched me when I used the remote to change the channels or turn on the TV.

I went into Netflix and found the Casper movie. His eyes didn't leave the TV. Although he was okay with the three ghost bullies, he almost fell off the lamp when the evil lady turned into a ghost. He was glad when she and her partner got their "comeuppance" as he called it. Then we watched *Ghostbusters I* and *II*, and the women's version. He was a bit mortified at all the bad ghosts, so I had to keep reminding him that it wasn't real. I kept telling him that a movie was meant to entertain like storytelling. It took a lot to finally get him to understand it, but I think he caught on. After a while, I told him that I had to leave to go see my uncle in the hospital. I put on *Ghost* before I left. I stayed away from the scary movies about ghosts—didn't want to give him ideas.

Uncle James looked a lot better, so I didn't stay very long. When I got back from the hospital, Zeke must have been having TV withdrawal. He flew down the stairs when he heard me come in.

"Would you please turn it back on?" Now I know how parents feel about how much TV their kids watch. I guess I didn't have to worry about Zeke's health or if he was getting enough exercise or fresh air. He got up on the lamp and bounced around like he just drank a gallon of Red Bull. He was that excited.

"Okay. But I'm going to go get something to eat next door." I didn't eat anything at the hospital. I had my mouth set on one of John's cheeseburgers. "I should be back before the end of the movie." I started my search for *Beetlejuice*.

"You going to see that nice boy next door?" His eyes never left the TV. Not even when I turned to glare at him. Not answering, I put on the movie, grabbed my coat, and went out the backdoor.

I let myself in through the back entrance of the Water's Edge. Tory was waiting on a table nearby. She wiggle-fingered hi and I wiggle-fingered hi in return. I headed back to the bar but no Tony or John. Tory approached the bar and lifted the counter gate and went behind it so she could face me.

"What's going on? Come back for round two?" she asked.

"Ha ha. I didn't have enough to eat before I . . ." Why am I explaining anything to Tory? "Where is everybody?"

"Well, I'm here," she emphasized by dramatically pointing her hot-pink-colored polished finger to herself. "Tony had to make a call. Probably to that woman he is seeing." She frowned when she said it. Good, so it isn't Tory. "John is in the kitchen. Do you want something to drink?"

"Oh no! I'm off that stuff for now. What woman?" I know I shouldn't be prying, but Tory will tell everything she knows.

"I wish I knew. You should see him when he leaves. He looks so good, girl!" She fanned herself with a menu. "Not that he don't look good anyway. I don't know who she is, but she better be worthy. That's all I'm saying." And of course that wasn't all she was saying. "If I wasn't going with my man, Don Don, girl please. I know he is my boss and all but really." She droned on and on until she saw someone waving at her. About then Tony came out of the little office behind the bar, and Tory went to take care of her customer.

"Hi, Billie. Do I need to put on a plastic smock?" He stuck his phone in his pocket and grinned at me.

"No, you don't have to put on a plastic smock." I used my extreme sarcastic voice. Then I said, "You think you're so funny." I kind of rolled my eyes and then chuckled. "I guess I had that coming. I have been a bit messy lately." I expelled a deep breath. "I am sorry. I've been having a little rough patch, but that's over. Pacts?" I held out my hand.

"Pacts." Tony shook it. We saw that in a John Wayne movie when we were kids. The four of us had been saying it ever since. About then my stomach growled loud enough that Tony heard it. "Maybe I should get John to make you a cheeseburger and fries." I nodded. "I'll be right back." I turned around on my bar stool and saw Uncle Pete in his regular booth. I got up and walked over.

"Hi, Uncle Pete." He saw me and stood up.

"Billie. If you aren't the prettiest girl in the Village." Then he looked around and said, "Except for my Birdie." We both laughed, and he gave me a warm bear hug, and then we both sat down in his booth. "How're you doing? We couldn't be happier that you are back. How's James? We are going to see him tomorrow. We were out of town the day he had the stroke, or we would have been there when it happened."

"Uncle James is doing pretty good. I know he hates being in the hospital and misses his cigars."

Uncle Pete chuckled. "I bet."

"Aunt Mae has been spending most of her time with him. She has a friend who lives near the hospital where she spends most of the nights that she doesn't spend with him. She doesn't like that long drive back and forth."

"Yeah, that's probably good because her eyesight isn't that good. She shouldn't be driving at all. She has hit a few things including our fence. I just fixed it and moved on." I didn't realize the struggles they had been facing here alone. I felt very guilty. "Don't beat yourself up. You may feel like Atlas, but the weight of the world doesn't rest on your shoulders or anyone's. So don't go drinking yourself crazy over it." He smiled and winked at me. I was so embarrassed. I dropped my head down, and he reached over and lifted my chin. "We all go a little crazy from time to time. You think you're the only one, shoot. Owning a bar, you see it happen all the time. Why, I remember one time when we were younger, Birdie got mad at me and threw a pot at me. Hit me too," he said indignantly. I started laughing. "Don't laugh. That woman has an arm. Should have played third base for the Tigers. Found out later that she was expecting John, and her hormones were all over the place. I was so upset I ran out of the house and came here. It was a Sunday, so we weren't open. I found Never sitting in the doorway. He looked so upset I had him come in. You wouldn't have known Never back then. He was a nice, clean-cut man who helped everyone and was well liked. Had great ideas for the Village. That wooden footbridge over the channel, he built that. Saved a lot of people steps."

Uncle Pete was interrupted when Tony came over to the booth with my cheeseburger and fries. He gave me a raspberry lemonade too. "Here you go. Tory told me you were on the wagon." He said with a big smile across his face. I frowned up my nose at him. "John said the sauce on top is a burgundy wine sauce with wild mushrooms and some kind of fancy cheese, but I don't remember what he said." He turned and looked at his father. "Dad, you want something?"

"Yes, a double scoop of raspberry chocolate chip ice cream in a waffle cone from the Big Dipper. Your mother somehow found out I was sneaking down there and told them not to let me have it. Bad days ahead when you are cut off from the Big Dipper."

Tony and I started laughing. "I'm not getting in the middle of that. No way," Tony said and shook his head. Just then John came over with a tray with food and a drink on it. It was a tuna sandwich and carrot sticks. He set the plate on the table in front of his father who looked at it sadly. Then he put a glass of water next to the plate.

"Mom called. Don't hate the messenger." He turned and went back into the kitchen.

Uncle Pete lifted the top piece of bread and peeked at it. He frowned and lowered the bread back down. He shook his head and said, "Prisoners eat better. I'm going to die a very hungry man." We all laughed. Tony went back to wait on some customers at the bar.

I leaned forward and I whispered to him. "If you don't tell, you can have half of my burger."

"Why Billie, I'm surprised and shocked at you." Uh-oh. I was just getting ready to apologize when he said. "You didn't offer me any of those fries. Do they come with the half?" He winked at me. I grinned at him.

"Yes, sir. But you can't tell."

"Deal." It was delicious, but I did feel a bit guilty about going against Aunt Birdie. We ate our food, and I caught him up on the family. I then prodded him to finish the story about Never.

"Oh yes, where did I leave off?" He had also finished his half and fries and was wiping his face with a paper napkin.

"Never was here in the doorway?" I tried to keep the nosiness out of my response, but this interested me to find out why Never was, well, Never.

"Oh, ah, so Never came in and he was a mess. He was crying, and I couldn't understand what he was saying. I told him that me and Birdie had a few words and offered him a drink. By the end of the night, we were both stinking drunk. But I found out why he was so upset. He had been married and divorced. They had a son. On that day, he had received a letter that had been forwarded a few times until it found him. Never moved around a bit after the divorce until he settled here. It was from his ex-wife. She told him that their son had been killed in a car accident. Never was never the same after that. He became the man he is now. Kind of broken. Somehow, we made it back to my house." He paused and took a drink of his water. He made a face and I laughed. "I don't know who was holding up who, and I don't know how we made it because we were through. Birdie took one look at both of us standing in the doorway and shook her head. She didn't say a word. She helped me put Never in one of the bedrooms. I sobered up a little and watched her take off his shoes and tuck him in. I love that woman." He started laughing. "She didn't tuck me in though. Nope, I followed her to our bedroom. She stopped me at the door and then threw a pillow and a blanket out in the living room. I said, "Oh the pillow and blanket you can throw in the living room but the pot you threw at me. Seriously?" I should have kept my big drunk mouth shut. She slammed the bedroom door in my face. I knew then our lives together were going to be a great journey." We both had tears in our eyes from laughing. "You are the only person I have ever told this story to. It must be the burgundy wine sauce that loosened my lips."

Tony watched his father and Billie laughing and talking. He also saw her share her burger and fries and smiled. John came out of the kitchen and walked behind the bar. He followed Tony's gaze over to the booth. He smiled at his brother and slapped him on his back. He walked back to the kitchen shaking his head.

CHAPTER 20

One of Uncle Pete's friends walked in and came over to where we were sitting. I knew his friend, and the three of us chatted for a minute or so. I decided that was my queue to get up. I slid out of my seat, gave Uncle Pete a kiss on the cheek, and walked toward the bar. As I got closer, Tony's cell must have vibrated in his pocket because he pulled it out. He looked at who was calling and smiled. He swiped it and held it to his ear and held his other finger to the other ear to hear better. His back was to me, so he didn't know that I had taken a seat at the bar. I laid my cell on the bar.

I heard him answer the phone. "Hi, honey." He was smiling. "Yes, I'll be there shortly. Just wrapping up a few things here. I've been thinking about how I hold you in my arms." I don't know why I should care but I did. I should be glad he is in love and thinking about holding someone in his arms, but it made me want to puke on him again. I couldn't hear a lot of what he was saying because he moved out of earshot. The last thing I heard before he disconnected was, "Don't worry. I'm here for you. I'll be there soon. Bye, honey." Then I saw him smile and say, "Tonight is the night." He turned and saw me sitting there probably looking as sour as I felt with my arms crossed in front of me.

"Was that Sexy Shirt?" I asked. He made a nervous kind of chuckle.

"You're not going to believe this, but that was just a friend." He smiled and started to say something else, but I interrupted.

"You're right. I'm not going to believe that." Just then my cell played "No Scrubs." Tony could see Pig Slop's name light up.

"You still let that jerk call you? What are you thinking? Block him." He looked kind of mad. I reached for my phone and swiped Ignore.

"That is none of your business." Yes, I had the nerve to say that after being all in his business. I got up and started walking away.

"Don't forget we got pacts," Tony shouted after me.

I kept walking. As I reached the backdoor of the Inn, I saw Tony run out to his car and leave.

Boys are dirtbags!

I got back in time to see the end of *Beetlejuice* with Zeke.

"How was dinner with that nice young man?" Zeke asked after the movie was over.

"I didn't have dinner with him. I actually had it with his father. Besides, he has a girlfriend, and I just got out of a terrible relationship and hate all men." Zeke looked horrified at that last comment. "Okay, that is a figure of speech. I don't hate all men. And Tony has been like my best friend all my life. I want him to have a wonderful woman that he can settle down with that doesn't buy him *Sexy shirts*." Zeke raised his eyebrows at that. I guess it was a lot for both of us to process. Zeke chose to change the subject.

"Would you show me how to use the changer?" he asked. He had the remote in his hand. It was so cute that he referred to it as the "changer" I couldn't tell him it was called a remote. What did it matter anyway?

"Sure." Then I slowly showed him how to use it. After a while he caught on. Zeke had mastered the "changer." I changed the setting to "parental control." I didn't want to warp his mind. I kind of felt responsible for his new TV addiction.

The next few nights I still couldn't sleep. It is just hard not to think about living with a ghost. During one of these sleepless nights, I got up and went to the kitchen for something to drink. I guess Zeke must have been in Private because I didn't see him. I got the orange juice out of the fridge and poured myself a glass. It wasn't that I was afraid of Zeke anymore. He seemed like a nice man, and I liked him. It was just weird, and I didn't sleep well at night. I don't know, maybe I was still a bit afraid. I opened the backdoor and walked out on the back porch.

The cool air went right through my flannel pajamas, and I shivered but didn't go back in. There was a full moon in the sky, and its reflection danced on the lake and I felt calm. I raised the glass up to my lips and was about to take a drink when something caught my eye. There it was again. I know I saw something moving down by the boathouse. I better get Never to set a live trap. It was probably a raccoon or possum. I think if it was a skunk, I would be able to tell without seeing it, if you know what I mean. Never can trap it and then move it to a new home out in the forest. I couldn't have it scaring the guest when the Inn was in full swing. I went back to bed and fell into a restless sleep.

I got up late that next morning with bags under my eyes and dragging around for lack of sleep. I came into the kitchen. Zeke was sitting on top of the refrigerator waiting for me. I guess he preferred high places. This morning I didn't even change out of my pajamas. I had my fuzzy pink slippers on that made a noise with each step that I drug across the wooden floor. Hey! What's that? I smelled the aroma of freshly brewed coffee. Zeke had watched me make coffee for the past couple of days and made me coffee this morning. He floated down from the refrigerator and got a cup off one of the hooks under the cabinet. He picked up the coffee pot and brought it all over to the table.

"Morning, Zeke. Thanks for making coffee." I mumbled through tight lips and barely opened eyes. He poured me a cup, and I watched as he disappeared into the refrigerator. I watched it rattle for a minute until the door popped open, and out he came with the half-and-half. He poured some into my cup. I guess he didn't want to struggle with the refrigerator door again because he put the half-and-half on the table and floated back up on the refrigerator. I could feel him looking at me from his perch. I picked up the coffee and started to drink it.

"Look, Billie, I'm a friendly ghost," Zeke said in his best Casper imitation. I spewed coffee all over the table, and we both laughed.

"I needed that. I was still a bit creeped out by sharing the Inn with a ghost. I don't know of any of my friends having one living with them. I don't know how all this will play out in the future, but I don't think either one of us will be leaving anytime soon. If it wasn't for you, I would never have known about the secret room in Private. I thank you for that."

"You should see the tunnel," Zeke said as he floated down and refilled my empty coffee cup.

"*What tunnel?* Is there a tunnel around here?" Now I'm awake. I got up and dumped the coffee in the sink. "Show me where there is a tunnel, and I think there needs to be a bit more transparency about anything else you know about around here."

"I just thought about it. My memory sometimes isn't as sharp as it was when I was a hundred," he said. "Grab a knife." I picked one up out of the draining rack and followed him as he headed in the direction of the basement door. Uh-oh! Why did it have to be in the basement? Here come the dragons and trolls. I blew out air and followed him down the steps. The basement was about the same footprint as the house above it. At least that's what I always thought. It hadn't gotten a lot of updates through the years because only the family used it. The washer and dryer were not far from the steps. There was a second refrigerator and a large freezer across from the washer and dryer. I glanced over at all the old furniture we had stored down there. There were some nice things that I wanted to come back and look through later. Aunt Mae didn't get rid of much through the years.

Deep in the basement, there was a small room with shelves where my aunt used to keep her canned goods that she put up every year. But it was cheaper and easier to just buy canned goods, so she stopped doing it. Zeke led me to the back of this cramped room, and sure enough, there was the same kind of locking mechanism camouflaged into the intricate carving of the molding just like the one in Private. You wouldn't notice it if you didn't know what you were looking for. I handed Zeke the knife, and he popped the latch open just like before. "This will need to be oiled too." He pressed the button, and the back swung open into darkness.

"I hate to sound like a baby afraid of the dark but . . ." Before I could finish, Zeke vanished and then reappeared shortly with my flashlight. He handed it to me. "B-b-before I g-g-go in th-th-there, w-w-where does this l-l-lead t-t-to?"

"It's been a long time since I've been in it, but I remember that Jackson wanted to have a way for our people to get out of the house without anyone seeing us. So I think it goes down to the lake. I just don't remember." The thought of me not knowing of a tunnel on our property must have temporarily shook the fear out of me.

"I've been over every inch of these grounds all my life, and I don't remember seeing any hidden openings."

"Well, there is a way to find out?" He tipped his head toward the tunnel. I was afraid he would say that. I turned on my flashlight and followed Zeke in. There was a stairway made of stone steps that descended to a narrow tunnel made out of many brick-sized blocks. The ceiling was round and only wide enough for one person to go through at a time. Although it was a bit musty, it was watertight. I played my flashlight along the walls to see if there was any graffiti or archeological symbols. Nope. No one had probably been in this tunnel for over a hundred years, and I'm the only living soul who knows about it. *This. Is. Awesome!* Boy, Georgie sure would love to know about this. But then everyone would know.

After a short walk, the tunnel ended, but to the right was another set of circular steps going up. Zeke headed up and disappeared. I gulped and followed. There were only about eight stairs before I had to crouch down as the ceiling became closer to my head. I stood on the highest step I could and swung my flashlight all around. I found the same locking device as the others and flipped it open. It wasn't stuck like the others and gave way to expose the button. I blew out air and pushed the button. Nothing. I pushed again. Hmmm. I put my empty hand up on the ceiling and gave it a push, and a trapdoor opened up. I hurried up the rest of the stairs and stepped out of the tunnel into a very small room that wasn't much bigger than a large closet. Where the heck was Zeke? I would feel better if he was with me, and about then he appeared.

"Where are we?" I asked. Zeke just beckoned me to follow him to a wall. He found a latch and carefully opened it, and we walked out. "Oh snap! This is the backroom in the boathouse." As Zeke closed the door, I looked carefully at it and saw that the mechanism was in fact there, but barely noticeable.

"Now I remember. Jackson didn't want the door to just pop open in case someone was in here. There is a little panel on the door so that you can see into this room. This had been a barn before. I guess they just built around it. When some of the slaves came through here, they stayed right here. I would bring them food, and after they rested for the night, Jackson would take them to the next stop in the wagon." He went back in, and I followed him so that he could show me. Sure enough, you had a great view of the full interior of the boathouse.

"This is awesome, Zeke. I can't believe I didn't know this was here. That no one knows this is here." I heard something in the boathouse. I beamed my flashlight to where I heard the noise. Nothing. Then I walked out into the main part of the boathouse and flipped on the light. I shut off the flashlight and looked all around. I saw nothing, but it was enough to give me the creeps. "I'll see you at the Inn," I yelled to Zeke as I ran to the boathouse door, turned off the lights, and stepped out into the sunshine. I took a few moments to appreciate my freedom and my beautiful view of the lake. I felt bad for the people who had to use that tunnel for their freedom and felt glad that Jackson Bradford was the kind of man he had been. And then I felt a pride that my family owns this piece of history. I needed to think about what I should do with this knowledge. Then I ran up to the Inn.

CHAPTER 21

After our tunnel adventure, I was curious if there were other surprises. Zeke couldn't think of any, but that doesn't mean there weren't. I continued to help Zeke catch up to modern technology. It was almost like teaching someone a new language. To Zeke's credit, he was a quick learner, and I think he liked this century. He loved listening to my Motown music with me. It was hard to explain that there weren't musicians hidden somewhere playing the music or a singer stashed in a closet. Believe me, he looked. He finally accepted that the music was coming from my phone. I caught him tapping his foot in time with the beat, grinning from ear to ear. He listened carefully to the lyrics, and some of them made him sad.

"That poor lady. That man broke her heart."

"It isn't real, Zeke. It's a song. They got paid lots of money to sing it."

"I still feel sorry for her." He slumped on his perch. Oh geesh. I can't have an unhappy ghost. I looked up "Because We're Happy" by Pharrell Williams and played it for him. It hooked him from the start and cheered him right up. He was grinning from ear to ear. He had me play it over and over again until he knew all the words. He would lip-sync them as he flew all over the room. Then he vanished for a minute and came back with the mop and broom. I guess he remembered my rendition of "Respect" with the mop. I took the mop from him and picked up one of Aunt Mae's straw hats that was hung on a nearby hook. He used the broom for his mic. We had to look silly, me with my mop mic and him with his broom and in his clothes from the eighteen hundreds. Well, I guess I looked silly because no one could see Zeke but me, but we were having a great time. I was all into the song, so I didn't notice that Zeke's broom had suddenly dropped, and he had disappeared. I had just worked a full twirl that ended with me looking at Tony. *OMG!* I have got to remember to lock those doors and to get a vicious guard dog because Zeke wasn't any help. Tony was standing there grinning at me. I snatched off the hat and threw down the mop. I pulled my cell out of my pocket and turned off the music.

He was standing in the doorway with his arms folded in front of him. "I did knock, but you didn't hear me. I'm glad to see you are doing better *and that you're happy.*" He sang the last part.

"I'm doing fine. *What* . . . do you want?" I plopped down on the leather chair nearby and put my feet up on the matching footstool.

"I came over to ask you if you wanted to ride with me to Traverse City. I need to pick up a part for my boat at West Marine. But if you're too busy working on your music tour, I certainly understand." He still had that smile on his face.

I gave him the squint eye and pursed my lips. "Does it include lunch at Apache Trout Grill?" I asked. I loved that place. I could just smell those fish tacos. Ump!

"You are a hard negotiator."

"Well, does it?"

"Of course."

"Okay, I'm in." I picked up Aunt Mae's hat and put it on my head. I sang, "Because I'm happy . . ." As I danced past Tony going out of the hallway door, he pulled it off and hung it on the coat hook.

Zeke watched as Tony helped Billie on with her coat and then as they walked out the door. He smiled to himself and picked up the mop and broom. He started humming, "Because I'm happy . . ." to himself as he floated up the stairs to Private.

The ride to Traverse City was nice. Tony knew that besides Motown, I loved Luther Vandross. Luther's greatest hits were playing on his radio. Tony's SUV was as clean as the day it rolled off the assembly line. That was kind of weird to me. I kept looking around.

"What are you looking for?" Tony asked after watching me look for a while.

"There isn't one old dried-up french fry, candy wrapper, empty water bottle, or used Kleenex to be found. Are you planning to sell this thing soon?"

He smiled, and I could see the corners of his eyes crinkle. It was nice.

"No, I had it detailed a week ago. Mom rode in it and said she wouldn't step foot in it again until it was clean." He didn't want to tell her that he had actually had it cleaned when he found out she was back.

"I guess I was so upset on the ride to the hospital I didn't notice. This is nice." I paused and after a little silence I said, "Ya know, I don't know why we argue so much. You have always been my best friend. I've had some . . . well, challenging days lately. I don't want you to think that I don't appreciate everything you do because I do. Appreciated it, I mean. I may not always express it, and I can be a bit messy, a little difficult," I was wondering if he was going to say something, "High maintenance? Cranky?" I blew out air. "Aren't you going to stop me?"

"Sorry, I was waiting for something that wasn't true. Never came." I looked over at him and rolled my eyes. "I meant it when I said I was glad you were here. I hope you have decided to stay this time." He paused for a moment and then said, "Some of the villagers are laying odds that you are going to leave at the end of the season." He looked over at me as if searching for a specific response before his eyes returned to the road. "So, are you going to stay? Don't stay because you are running away from something or because you feel a sense of duty. It will never make you happy, Billie."

I laid my head back against the headrest and looked up at the ceiling. I thought about the Inn, Pig Slop, Aunt Mae and Uncle James, and Zeke, and then I looked over at Tony. "This is my home now. I'm staying because I love it here." Tony looked over at me, and I looked at him. "And for camel cake."

"That's my girl." Tony smiled as he looked back at the road and started singing "Power of Love" with Luther.

It was late in the afternoon when we got back. It was a really nice trip and we got along for once. I was smiling as Tony dropped me off at the Inn. I came in the door and heard a TV on in the common room. Clearly, Zeke had mastered the "changer." Intending to go to my room first, I walked past the doorway to the common room. I peeked in as I walked by. I suddenly stopped in my tracks and backed up. Zeke was dressed up like an old cowboy: big cowboy hat, vest, chaps, boots, and gun belt. I could even hear his spurs jingling. If that wasn't weird enough, he was in black and white. I looked over at the TV, and it was playing an old John Wayne picture.

"How do I look?" Zeke said, smiling at me. My mouth was open, but words didn't come out.

"Wow," was all I could finally manage to say. I must know the coolest ghost ever! I tried not to laugh when I saw him later that day in green tights and swishing a sword around. "Let me guess. You were watching Robin Hood." He nodded his head and went on with his sword fight. Evidently it wasn't the cool Kevin Costner, Russell Crowe, or Leonardo DiCaprio version. Nope, it was the Errol Flynn one. He seemed to really like the action movies. I'm so glad that I put on that parental viewing because I would hate to suddenly walk in on Freddy Kruger, Chucky, or the clown from *It*.

Zeke put away his sword and brought out his bow. He pulled an arrow out of his quiver and took aim. Just then my cell phone rang and started Zeke. His arrow misfired through the wall and disappeared. He shrugged his shoulders in apology. I answered it and it was Momma. Zeke studied me while we talked, so I switched on the speaker. He looked all over the phone looking for Momma. After I hung up, Zeke asked, "How do those people get in there, and why can't I see them?" He was still dressed as Robin Hood.

"What do you mean?"

"Inside that little thing."

I always took the cell phone for granted. I really didn't know why it worked and didn't care as long as it did work. But now, it called for some explanation. "It's kind of like the TV except it is people talking in real time." I wasn't going to go into all the other things a cell phone does.

"Huh?"

I took a deep breath and blew out air. "Okay, it is something you use to talk to someone without them being with you. Like I would love to talk to my sister right now, but she is in the city, and I am here." To help him understand, I called Georgie and put her on speaker so that he could hear her.

"Hello?" Georgie answered after two rings. Zeke almost jumped out of his ectoplasmic green tights and feathered cap. He answered, "Hello." Then his puzzled face turned into a smile.

"Hi, Georgie. How are things going?" I said.

"Good. I'm glad you called. Did I tell you about Marcus's new job?" Georgie went on with details that would make Mrs. Baits happy.

"It's like she is here, but I can't see her. Like I was before you could see me," Zeke said. But Georgie couldn't hear him and talked right over him. "But no one could hear me either so I guess it's not the same." I let Zeke work that out on his own.

Then she started talking about people she worked with, the girls and their ballet classes. About then I put on my mental screensaver and watched Zeke's face during all this. He was fascinated and hung on every word. During the conversation, his regular clothes materialized.

"Georgie, would you let Billie get a word in?" We heard Marcus yell in the background. I love my brother-in-law. I couldn't have picked a better man for Georgie or a better father for the girls. I could just imagine Georgie giving Marcus the stink eye. I smiled.

"Sorry, Billie, I guess I did go on for a while. I just miss you." I didn't realize until she said it that I missed her too.

"Oh don't go all mushy on me. Just come up when you can. You have to see all the things I have done to the Inn." We talked a bit about that, and then she promised to come up and bring Marcus and the girls for Fourth of July weekend. I didn't have much more to tell her other than I am living with a ghost, Private is a secret room and there is a tunnel, but that was so last week I didn't mention it. We said our goodbyes and hung up.

Zeke hungered for more and asked me to call someone else only he said would I "tap someone else." I showed him how to find my contacts. I have to give him credit, he kept trying. I guess when you have endless time on your hands, that is what you do. After a few hundred tries, I figured out that Zeke needed to be able to touch the screen. I had a pair of cell phone gloves that Georgie gave me for Christmas a year ago. I went and got them and had Zeke put on one. Zeke was finally able to get to one of my contacts on his own and knew how to "tap" them. As I watched him pull up a pizza place at home, I felt like Henry Higgins in *My Fair Lady* when Liza mastered "The rain in Spain falls gently on the plains." It felt good to teach Zeke something he would never use.

I felt he could move on to something else, so I went and got my laptop. I powered it up and put in my password. It was also a touchscreen, and he could maneuver some of it as well. I showed him Facebook, and then I went to check my e-mails. My friends from the city sent me a bunch of YouTube links. Big mistake, because I found a number of them that showed my incident in the Atrium of the Embassy Suites.

"You, you, you, *Pig Slop!*"

"What movie is this?" Zeke asked, laughing so hard I thought he would fall off the floor lamp. "This is too funny. And that girl looks just like you." I slammed my laptop closed and said, "Class dismissed." I left the room. I could still hear him laughing as I headed back in the direction of my room.

I stopped in the hallway and set my phone on the little hall table. I looked at myself in the mirror that hung above the table. "What have I gotten myself into? Is my hair growing white?" I silently asked my reflection as I looked through my roots. I went to my room and threw myself on my bed. I yawned and must have dozed off because I was suddenly jarred awake when I heard the Temptations singing "Can't Get Next to You." I got up and started hunting for my cell. I don't know why I can't keep up with it, TV remotes or socks. All of today's training had panned out because Zeke found it and had answered it sort of with my glove. He was dressed like Spider-Man, and he shot it at me in a web. I said a silent "Thank you" and saw that it was Aunt Mae. Zeke smiled and nodded his head. Pleased with himself he disappeared.

"Hi, Aunt Mae."

"Hi, Billie. Good news. They are going to release James in a couple of days."

"That's wonderful, Aunt Mae. I have your rooms all ready for you and Uncle James. I've even bought some things on Amazon for Uncle James to help him with his recovery." I had looked at a lot of products for someone who was recuperating from an illness.

"Oh Billie, I am sorry that you went through so much trouble because your uncle and I are going to move into the Ivy House." The Ivy House was a small cottage that had been included as part of the property purchased with the Inn. Through the years there had been many renters who lived in it, but for the last two years, it had been vacant. "If we are at the Inn, James is going to try to run things. I need him away from it so that we can be fully retired. I'm not saying that we won't help you if you need us, but I have to get him well."

"I will get everything ready at the Ivy House. Never is going to help with the chores around here, and there is a girl who is working at the Bait Shop who came by a few days ago asking about a job as a part-time housekeeper. Will that be okay with you, Aunt Mae?"

"Girl, you are running things now. Those are your decisions, not mine." She chuckled as she said it.

"Well, I guess I have a part-time housekeeper and groundskeeper."

"I don't know the girl, but I think Never is a good choice. He's honest, trustworthy, and a hard worker. You won't be sorry."

"Her name is Suzy something or other, and she said that Mrs. Baits would vouch for her."

"Well, if Josephine will vouch for her, you got a good housekeeper. Now don't do too much. I'll keep you posted on when we are coming home. By the way, when you move us out, you need to move you in. That is your home now."

We hung up, and I got up and walked up to the attic and knocked on Private. Zeke poked his head out and said, "Hi. Want to come in?"

"Why not?" Actually, I could think of a thousand scary reasons why not, but I went in anyway.

CHAPTER 22

It looked like Zeke had been busy cleaning. The place looked spotless, not like it looked before. There were no cobwebs or dust anywhere. It no longer looked like a haunted house in a scary movie. He had a few kerosene lamps lit, and I thought to myself I am going to have to figure out how to run lights safely in here.

"I thought if you were gonna visit me in here from time to time, I should fix it up. How do you like it?"

"This is really nice, Zeke. Mr. Bradford must have really loved his son to make this cool room for him."

"Cool. Is it cold in here? I have no way of knowing."

"Cool means nice. He made a nice room for his son."

"He didn't make it for his son. He made it for me. And others like me."

"What do you mean?"

"He had been an abo . . . abo . . ."

"Abolitionist?"

"Yes, ma'am. He was always concerned that someone would come for me."

"Oh, I am sorry, Zeke. I forgot that you were around back then."

"Yes. Me and Jackson grew up on a plantation together and were best friends. Our mommas were as close as a slave and master could be. My momma watched Jackson like he was my brother, and I found out later why. I was the only child my momma had, but like I said, she took care of him like he was her son. There were a few times Jackson's father wanted to sell me, but old Mrs. Bradford wouldn't let him. His father was one of the old Southerners who liked slavery, but Jackson didn't think it was right. There were times when he spoke up to his father about how slavery was wrong

and cruel. When Mrs. Bradford died from the fever, Jackson was a young man. His father sent him away to school. While he was away, his father sold me to Mr. Jamison. My momma cried and begged, but he sold me anyway. Mr. Jamison had a mean overseer. Both were evil men who treated all the slaves terrible. All of us were beaten often, and one time I was beaten so bad I almost died. It was around that time that Jackson showed up one night and carried me right out of my sick bed. He stole me right off the Jamison plantation. He hid me in a wagon that had a false bottom, and we headed north. I was afraid for us both. They didn't like white men who helped slaves and would hang us both if we were caught. Jackson risked his life for me. Jackson never left my side unless it was to go into town for food. We hid in the woods during the day and moved north during the night. We almost drowned crossing a large river. I was so sick and hurting there were times I must have passed out because when I woke up one morning, I was in a different wagon and there was an older white lady with Jackson. Her name was Miss Haviland, but she insisted that both me and Jackson called her Laura. She took care of my wounds and fed me. I must have been a mess because one time when she was taking care of my wounds, a tear dropped down on me. She kept promising me that she would get us to safety. Jackson told me that she was well-known by the bounty hunters and slave masters for helping slaves escape. They were looking for her too, but they weren't looking for a white man and his mother. We made it into Michigan, and a little later, we met up with a Negro woman named Truth. We finally ended up here. Jackson had money that his momma left him and got into the lumber business. He married a nice lady who was sickly, especially after the baby. There were white people who called themselves 'friends.' They took care of me and got me well again. They helped Jackson build this fine home. They built that tunnel too."

"Quakers probably. They called themselves 'the Society of Friends.' I heard there were many in the area who were against slavery."

"I guess so. Then one day, Mr. Jamison's men showed up here. Jackson saw them riding up on horses and told me to hide. I barely got hidden before they busted through the door and demanded that they search the house. But they didn't find me. I was in a secret room. One of them said they should burn the house down, but some of the friends had arrived. Although they wouldn't fight, they didn't have to. There were so many of them, Mr. Jamison's men just got back on their horses and left."

"How terrible. What about your family? Didn't you have one?" He looked so sad then, I wish I hadn't asked.

"Yes, I had a wife, Bessie, and two little children. They all died from the sickness, and I was the only one left. It was probably better that they died then. There were times when I was a slave and wished I had died with them. At least they were free. I never found any of them on this side."

I saw pain and loneliness in his eyes and tried to change the subject. "But why are there so many wooden toys"—I pointed all around the room—"if he didn't mean for this to be a playroom."

"I was a toymaker. I made toys for all the children. When Bradford left and I was here alone, I just kept making toys. One day he came and gave me some papers. He told me to sign them. I could read and write because old Mrs. Bradford taught me. I started to read them, and he stopped me. He looked me in the eyes and said, 'Look, Zeke, I found out that you are my brother. We have the same daddy, the same blood. I was planning on giving you this house anyway, but now, knowing that you are my real brother, I am so happy to be able to do this. Sign this, and no one can take this away from you.' I signed the papers without reading them, and he left. My momma never told me. Even when I asked. I guess she was afraid that if Mrs. Bradford found out, she would change towards us. So when I . . . died"—he stumbled on that word again—"I stayed here."

I wanted to ask him more but thought maybe another time would be better. We looked at all the little hand-carved toys that Zeke made. Each had intricate detail and craftsmanship. It reminded me of something.

"Zeke, did you carve the little hidden panel in the desk in the office?" That wiped away that gloomy look he just had and was replaced with a huge smile.

"Yes, I sho' did. In fact, I made the desk. I would spend a lot of time with those nice people. They made beautiful furniture. They let me hang around and watch at first, then they let me help. I learned a lot from them. I started making my own furniture."

"I almost forgot why I came up here in the first place. As you know there will be a lot of people here as guests of the Inn." I eased into it. "I am going to need help. I just want to make sure that you don't scare them away." He looked insulted.

"No one can see or hear me 'cept you. I wouldn't do that anyway."

"Great, I'm going to the store to pick up a few groceries and to talk to a girl who works there. She is hopefully going to be our housekeeper. Then

I'm going to talk to a man we call Never. He is going to help around here too." I paused for a moment and then said, "Thank you for sharing your story with me, Zeke. It is one thing to read about this in a book or to see a movie about it. It's another to have someone who lived through it tell it. Thank you, Zeke." If I could have kissed him on the cheek, I would have. I pushed the button to let myself out. I thoughtfully looked back at Private. Zeke owned my heart, and I was glad that my Inn came with a ghost.

Jasper had it all planned. The next day, he drove through town with his window down, smiling and waving at the few people who were out walking. He pulled into the Cut Above's parking lot at his normal time to open the store. He made a big show of it in case anyone was looking. He unlocked the door and stepped inside. He hurried out to the backdoor and broke out the back window with a piece of pipe he had found. He carefully wiped off the piece of pipe and threw it out in the back. He left the backdoor standing wide open. He waited about ten minutes, and then called Pudgy.

. "I've been robbed," he yelled into the phone.

"Hang on, Jasper. What did you say?"

"I said I've been robbed. I came in and the register was empty. I looked around and a window is broken and the backdoor was standing open. Just get your butt over here."

Not long after Pudgy was at the Cut Above taking Jasper's statement and looking the place over. He was a short black man, and even though he was inside, he kept on his dark sunglasses. His shirt was too small and his exposed belly hung over his belt. The belt held multiple items, but the most obvious was his pistol. The hem of his pants was too short, and all together everything made him look a bit comical and typical.

"And where is Rachel?"

"She left a few days ago to go to her mother's. She won't be back for a while."

"She wouldn't know anything about this, would she?"

"I'm pretty sure she wouldn't have to bust in and done this. No, she didn't. She didn't know I put five hundred thousand dollars in the register. She left yesterday to go see her mother in Kentucky. We just took it out of the bank a few days ago. No one knew I put that money in the register. I think it was just a vandal who got lucky, and I know who it is. Never did it."

"What makes you think it was Never?"

"He was skulking around my wife a few days ago, and I had to throw him out of here."

"Did you touch anything?"

"Well, heck yeah. This is my store, so I've touched everything. I looked in the register so that's how I know the money is missing. Then I noticed the backdoor standing open and the broken window."

"Just close for the day so that we can investigate it."

"But I need to be open."

"Do you want to be open or find who has your money?"

"Okay."

"I'll need to speak to Rachel too."

"I'll give you her number. Like I said, she went to visit her mother." He gave Pudgy the number.

"I'll need to take your prints and eventually Rachel's so that I can rule those out. Since she is out of town, do you have something of hers with her prints on it?"

"How about her hairbrush?"

"That will probably work for now, but I will need to talk to her eventually."

"No problem." Well, this was working out well. Yes, this was going to work.

CHAPTER 23

The next morning, I walked over to the Bait Shop. I could see Mrs. Baits behind the counter. "Hi, Mrs. Baits. How are you doing?"

"Doing fine, Billie. How's James?"

"He's coming home soon, or actually he and Aunt Mae are going to move to the Ivy House. Aunt Mae thought it would be better."

"Yes, it probably would be. So glad he is doing well. The Ivy House is so cute, and I thought about making an offer on it, but I'm glad now that I didn't."

"Well, the reason I'm here is, well, I was wondering if . . ." Oh boy, I'm not doing well.

"If you wonder if Suzy can help you there and at the Inn, I will definitely vouch for her. She is a hard worker. I am so blessed to have her." She lowered her voice and said, "That Sandy is so lazy. If I hadn't known her mother and had been her friend to the end . . ."—she looked sad for a moment—". . . and if she didn't need a job, I think I would have fired her by now." She stopped her whispering and said, "That is if you don't mind that Suzy comes without any formal documents. She was homeless, poor thing, before coming here and lost all of her information. She is working on getting it, but it is a slow process, I guess. I'm letting her stay in one of the small rental cottages that I've been using for storage. It needs a lot of work, but she didn't mind, and it's only temporary until she can get back on her feet. She is a very hard worker, and if I didn't think she could work here and over at your Inn, I wouldn't say so. Besides, come the summer I won't need her because I always have made a point of hiring a couple of the high school children while they are out on summer vacation. It teaches them responsibility. I'm stuck with Sandy," she said sadly.

"Thank you. That will work out great. The summer is my busy time. Is Suzy here? I'd like to talk to her."

"Yes, she is in the back."

"Thank you. I'll go find her." I headed to the back of the store. I passed Sandy, who had been obviously eavesdropping. She rolled her eyes at me as I passed.

"Hi, Sandy." I faked a friendly sound to my voice. I think she knew it because she gave me a fake friendly answer.

"Hi, Billie. Wish I had more time to chat, but I'm very busy." She clicked her hot-pink fingernails and rolled her eyes again. There must be a sale on hot-pink fingernail polish. Sandy just stood there watching me as I walked to the back of the store.

I found Suzy up on a ladder reaching for a large box of toilet paper.

"Hey, Suzy, just how were you going to get that safely down on the floor from up there?" I asked with a chuckle. I reached up to take the box as she handed it down to me.

"Good question." She smiled back as she descended the ladder.

I jumped right in. "I would like to hire you. I spoke to Mrs. Baits as you suggested, and she only had great things to say about you. I need help immediately because my aunt and uncle are going to go live at the Ivy House." I saw her look confused and went on to say, "It's a rental house that our family owns that has been sitting empty for a few years. They are going to move there. My uncle has been in the hospital after having a stroke and needs to have a stress-free place to live. I need it cleaned up for starters, and then, when the Inn opens in a few weeks, I will need someone to help me clean the rooms full time. Mrs. Baits said you would be available. Are you still interested?" I took a deep breath and hoped I didn't sound as needy as I felt.

"That sounds great. How much is the pay?" Smart girl. We talked about her pay and that if things worked out, we may be able to do more. But she was going to have to get her identification records as soon as possible. I didn't want any trouble with Uncle Sam. I had enough of jail.

Suzy and I finished our business, and I left her to her tasks. I picked up a handled basket and went around the store and picked up the few things I needed. I didn't see Sandy anywhere, so I guess she was mopping the floor or cleaning out a shelf of expired cans, *not*. I paid Mrs. Baits and left the store. I dropped off what I bought, put away anything that needed refrigeration, and then got in my bug and started out to Never's camper.

As I passed the Cut Above, I saw Pudgy's police car parked in front of the store's door. *Probably grabbing a side of beef for lunch*, I thought to myself and giggled.

I drove out to Never's camper. It was back down a secluded wooded road that broke out into a clearing. There were woods surrounding the clearing. The camper sat mostly on sand, but there was enough dead vegetation around to make it look that much more run-down. The outhouse needed repair as well. There were old rusty pieces of odds and ends of equipment long past usefulness all over the yard. Some were so decayed you couldn't tell what they once were. There was an old kitchen chair made of rusty chrome tubing and ripped green vinyl that sat by the door. It tilted slightly to the left from lots of use. Everything carried the depressed characteristics of its owner. It made me even more determined to help Never.

The camper had once been white with a light-green stripe running horizontally through the middle, but now the white looked yellowish with wear, and the green had faded. I stepped up on a wooden box that was a makeshift porch. It gave a little under my weight. I knocked on the door that was made from wood paneling that wasn't part of the original camper design. The regular door probably fell off and was an artifact somewhere in Never's rusty graveyard.

I could hear something being moved across the floor close to the door, and then Never pushed open the door. I had to step back off the wooden box so that the door could swing free.

"Hi, Billie."

"Hey, Never. Can I talk to you?"

"Do you want to come in?" He sounded so surprised. I guess no one comes to visit him here. I can understand why, and I think I would feel more at ease in the room behind Private than I would here. But I felt something for Never, maybe empathy, maybe sympathy, just something that made me want to suck it up and pretend I was entering the Taj Mahal.

"Yes, is that okay? I don't want to impose." He grunted and moved further inside to let me in. He went over to a matching kitchen chair like the one outside. I mean really matching. Equally as rusty and ripped. He made a motion of wiping it off with his bare hand and pointed for me to sit. I sat down and looked around.

"It's a dump, I know," he said as he pulled up a footstool and sat down on it. He didn't say it in a sad way but more as a fact. I didn't know what to say to that. I was hoping that I didn't need a tetanus shot from sitting on this chair. I tried to act like I didn't notice how there was junk everywhere. Never must have collected his treasures from everyone's trash. But among all the junk there was a wide bookshelf filled with lots of books.

"I see you like to read. I do too. Do you have a favorite author?"

"Not really. A beggar can't be a chooser." I looked away. I didn't want all of our conversations to be depressing. I looked at the table next to me, and my eyes rested on the Alaska book that I had given him. I noticed that he had bookmarked many places. I reached over and picked it up.

"Did you like this book?"

At that, he came over and sat next to me on a footstool. He took it from me and opened it to the first bookmark.

"I worked at a camp here," he pointed to a photograph in the book. His whole face changed. He started thumbing through the book and showing me places he had been and what he had done while there. Never had a very colorful life in Alaska. He told about the people and how they lived. He made some of the villages sound like the old TV series *Northern Exposure*. He said that is what attracted him to the Village years ago. Then he did something rather unexpected. He smiled, or maybe it was gas, because it disappeared quickly.

"Tomorrow, would you come and help Suzy, the girl from the Bait Shop, clean out and fix up the Ivy House? I will need help moving their personal things over to the Ivy House. I need that done as soon as possible. After that is all done, I would like for you to help me move my stuff into Uncle James and Aunt Mae's rooms and some other things around the Inn." I leaned closer to him and said, "I need your help."

He looked me straight in my eyes as if to see if it was all a lie. Seeing that it wasn't, his face changed to one of hope. "I will be glad to help you. I will go to the Ivy House now. I always admired that property." He got up from his stool, and I carefully got up from the kitchen chair of death. We both got into our vehicles and headed for the Ivy House.

CHAPTER 24

As we walked around the outside the Ivy House, I pointed out things that needed to be done, and Never suggested other things. I shouldn't have assumed that just because he didn't do any upkeep of his camper he didn't know how to maintain property. We walked up to the open porch, and I pulled keys out of my pocket. I unlocked the door. It smelled musty, and it was dark inside. I made a mental note to take some of the extra curtains and linens we had at the Inn and have Never bring them here. I also needed Never to take one of the double beds in the attic room apart and bring it here. It was this critical thinking that helped me develop a list for me for Never and for Suzy. I gave Never his list, and without a word, he started on it.

I left him to his tasks and went back to the Bait Shop. I explained where the Ivy House was to Suzy and asked her if she could go there as soon as possible. I went over her list of things to do and said that the man she met the other day named Never who would be working with her. She suddenly looked at me.

"Listen, he is a very nice man who got stuck. I hope you don't have a problem working with him."

"Oh no, I am glad for the work. If I can work with Sandy, I can work with anyone." We both laughed. I had to agree with her on that. I told her I would send cleaning supplies over with Never on one of his trips back and forth, and they would be there when she got there. She agreed, and with that, I went back to the Inn to start on my list.

Never went by with things to go to the dump and probably things he was going to keep. He came back shortly and gathered up all the things I had ready, including all the things I had bought on Amazon. Suzy, who had just finished her shift at the store, walked over.

"If it's okay with you, I would like to ride over to the house with you. I don't have a car." She said to Never.

"Sure, sure." Never moved a lot of junk he had on the passenger seat and threw it in the back. Suzy climbed in, and they both rode off to the Ivy House. I suddenly remembered that I needed Never to set a trap out by the boathouse. I needed to remember to write that on a new list I was working on for Never.

Chief Pudgy was coming out of the Cut Above when he saw Never and the young lady who worked at the Bait Shop drive by. He saw them turn up a road that he knew led to the Ivy House. He got in his car and drove over. Never was pulling some yard tools out of his truck when he saw Pudgy pull up.

"Hi, Chief."

"Hi, Never." Pudgy looked up to the sky searching for his next sentence. "I hear you and Jasper had a squabble. He said that you were attacking his wife so that you could take money from the register. He says he got there just in time to throw you out." Pudgy waited for Never to respond.

Never looked sad. "I would never attack that poor lady. She has enough of a problem being married to him."

"Well, that's what Jasper said. He said he is pretty sure you robbed him. He had five hundred thousand dollars in the register. It was Rachel's inheritance."

"What?" Never looked shook. He wasn't sure what to say.

"I need you to come to the station so that we can take your prints. I'll bring you back here afterwards. Come on, Never." Never started walking over to Pudgy's car and started to get in the front. "Would you mind getting in the back?" Never opened the backdoor and got in. Suzy watched and listened from inside the house behind the curtained front window that had been open. She shook her head and sat down. She hung her head down and cried.

A little bit later, Pudgy returned with Never. Never slowly got out of the backseat and walked over to his yard tools and got to work. The wind was clearly removed from his sails. Suzy heard them pull up and went to the kitchen. She poured a glass of lemonade over ice and waited until Pudgy left, and then she took it out to Never.

"Here. I'm sure it will be okay." Never looked sadly up at her. "Look, I believe you." Then she walked back into the house. Never didn't know why, but he felt a lot better because of what Suzy said.

The two worked hard and silently, each within their own thoughts. When they felt they had accomplished enough for the day, they climbed into Never's truck. He dropped her off at her cottage and decided to go see Billie.

I had found more things to be taken over to the Ivy House and had them sitting on the porch when Never pulled up. As he got out of the truck, I said, "Hi, Never. I found more things to go over to the Ivy House. I hope you don't mind taking them over. It can wait until tomorrow. I know you must be tired. Have you eaten? Would you like to be my guest at the Water's Edge?" All the time I was talking I noticed how upset he looked. "Please come inside to the kitchen, Never. I will ask Roger to deliver our food and you can rest. I'm sure you're tired." I made the call, and we both walked up to the front porch and went inside. The silence was so thick I had to break it. "How is it coming? I think Aunt Mae and Uncle James are in for a pleasant surprise." We went into the kitchen, and both sat down at the table. That was when Never finally broke his silence.

"I may not be able to help anymore," Never said sadly.

"Why not? If the work is too much—"

"No. I think I will be arrested." He saw the shocked look on my face and said, "You have to believe me. I didn't do it. I would never take something that wasn't being thrown away or given to me."

Puzzled, I asked, "What are you talking about, Never?" He told me about Jasper, Rachel, and what happened today with Pudgy. About then we heard a car door slam. I signaled Never to sit tight while I go see who it is. The first thing I saw through the window is Pudgy's squad car. I went back to the kitchen.

"Never, quietly go up the back stairs. I don't know if Pudgy is here for you, but just in case I want you to hide until we can get this all straightened out." Never looked at me like I threw him a lifeline and did as he was told. I calmly sat at the kitchen table and waited. Soon Pudgy was in the doorway looking around.

"Hi, Billie. I see Never's truck out front. Is he here?"

I looked all around the kitchen and said, "I don't see him."

"C'mon, Billie, don't be like that. I just need to bring him in for some questioning. His truck is out front, so I know he must be here."

"Yep, he had some trouble with it and left on foot. Said he'd be back in the morning for it." I crossed my fingers behind my back. I've been to jail so I'm an ex-hardened criminal now myself. Actually, it felt more like I was lying to Pudgy, not the law. I know that is splitting hairs, but that is how I felt. Just then Roger came in through the backdoor with the food delivery.

"Hi, Pudgy. Hi, Billie. I got your two burgers and fries. John put a new sauce on them that he has been perfecting." I ran over to him with my purse and got money out to pay him.

"Thanks, Rog. I'm sure these will be great. Boy am I hungry." I gave him a tip and ushered him out the back. Pudgy was looking around, opening and closing doors.

"Do you have a search warrant?" I asked.

"Just looking for ghosts." He started laughing. I started laughing too because Zeke was sitting on the counter right in front of him dressed as Jack Sparrow, sticking his tongue out at him. "Look, I'm not arresting him, I just have to ask him some more questions. Turns out the locket that was in the register belonging to Rachel had Never's fingerprints on it," he said loud enough so that it could be overheard by Never. "Rachel hasn't made it to her mom's, so she may have taken the money. So, I'm not saying he's guilty of anything, but I have to do my job."

"Well, go do it someplace else. I need to eat my dinner."

"That's quite a lot of food for a little woman." He tipped his hat. "Enjoy." Then he raised his voice again and said loud enough to be heard upstairs, "Tell Never that I'll catch up with him later." With that, he walked out and drove off.

"You can come down now, Never." He came down the steps and looked more miserable than when he went up them.

"I didn't do it. She broke the chain on her locket and dropped it. I picked it up for her. I forgot all about it until I heard him say my prints were on it. I'm going to jail for sure, and I didn't do it."

"Don't worry. Things will work out. Here, have your burger." We ate in silence.

After Never left, I tried to figure out what I could do to help him. I didn't believe for one minute that he would steal anything. Look at his place, his truck, his clothes. That wasn't the lifestyle of anyone who was a thief. He would have to have something to show for it. Besides, I could just tell that he wouldn't do such a thing. Captain Zeke Sparrow was sitting on the refrigerator. He must have just watched *Pirates of the Caribbean.*

"I just don't believe he did it," I said to him.

"I don't think he did it either. When he was upstairs, he looked so sad I thought he was going to cry. I know a thief when I see one, and he isn't one," said Zeke.

"I want to help him. I just don't know how yet." But I will think of some way.

CHAPTER 25

The next morning I woke up late. I had stayed awake most of the night wondering how to help Never. It was a good thing because it took my mind off that crap with Pig Slop. Yes, that tortured my mind from time to time but not because I still cared about him. I hated that I got sucked in by him. I felt stupid and made a fool out of myself with him. About then I heard my ringtone play, Marvin Gaye and Tammy Terrell's "You're All I Need to Get By."

"Hi, Tony. What's up?"

"Have you eaten breakfast yet? I know it's late, but I thought we could walk to the Over Easy. I've got a taste for Martha's cinnamon almond French toast."

Hmm. I've kind of sworn off the breakfast burritos. "That sounds great. Give me twenty minutes, and I will meet you out on the front porch."

"Sounds good to me."

I showered and put on clean clothes but then changed them to something that made me feel prettier. I pulled on my Converses. I don't know why I was so picky about what I put on because it was just Tony, and he was used to seeing me in my normal jeans and T-shirts. He has also smelled my puke-infested T-shirt too, which reminded me. I pulled his Sexy shirt off the top of the laundry basket of clean clothes and folded it. I stuck it in my purse. I looked in the mirror and pulled my curls back into a loose ponytail. Happy with what I saw, I headed out of my bedroom. As I passed the common room, I saw Zeke up on the lamp. As usual he was in character. He must have just watched *Beetlejuice* again. He was channel-surfing.

"Good morning, Zeke."

"Good morning, Billie."

"Don't bother to fix me coffee this morning. I'm going out to breakfast."

"With Tony?" He actually hiked his transparent brows up and down a couple of quick times.

"Yes, why do you always say it like that? He is like my brother."

"Sure. Sometimes you have to see what is in front of you."

Now I have a zen-like Beetlejuice ghost. "I told you, Tony has some secret girlfriend he is seeing." Even though we seem to always argue, I feared our relationship would change when Tony was ever serious about someone. I didn't want that to happen. I had a scare with John when he got married, but that didn't last. Now I was sour. Thanks, Zeke.

When I opened the door and walked out on the large front porch, there was Tony sitting on the porch swing. The sun was filtering in on him, and it almost made him look like he was glowing. He was dressed casually but still looked like he could be on a movie set.

"Good morning, Billie. You look beautiful."

"You too. I mean you look g-g-great." Did I stutter? What is wrong with me? I walked over and sat next to him on the porch swing.

"I guess you heard about Never." When one works behind the bar in this small town, word gets around.

"He didn't do it."

"I don't think he did it either. It's not like Never. I've been around him all my life, and I just don't see it. Now Jasper, I wouldn't doubt it."

"But you know Pudgy can't find his butt with both hands. I bet that Jasper took the money himself. He is such a lowlife."

"I agree. Never has always been a good guy, but maybe he just lost it. I heard he was awfully mad at Jasper. Look, it will be okay. I'm with you. I would rather believe Never over Jasper any day." He put his hand under my chin and guided my face until we were looking eye to eye. I could see, behind Tony, Zeke's head sticking out of a flower pot. He was making a kissing motion with his lips. I broke away.

"Come on, let's go get our grub on." I stood up and started walking to the screen door. With my back to Tony, I gave Zeke a stern look as I passed him. I swatted at him and he disappeared. Then remembered Tony was sitting there so I acted like I was swatting at a bug even though it was too cold for insects.

"Ah, spiderweb." I'm becoming such an accomplished liar.

"Hey, come here a second," Tony said. I turned and walked back over and sat down.

"Yes," I said as I pulled my gloves out of my pocket and started pulling them on.

Tony jumped up and ran out the door yelling, "The last one there has to buy."

I got up laughing and ran after him. "Cheater!"

CHAPTER 26

Never liked to walk out deep into the woods behind his camper. It helped him clear his mind. He liked to look over the pipeline that ran through the forest and check for leaks like he once did for a living. Most of the pipeline was buried, but there were some places where he knew the pipes were exposed. Helicopters would periodically fly over, checking for leaks. Now the pipelines are checked via remote sensors that track any pressure changes or flow rates, but not when Never worked the pipelines in Alaska.

He headed back to his camper. He couldn't quite see it yet, but he knew the woods so well that he knew he was close. But then he heard a noise. It didn't sound like forest noises. This one was out of place. Curious as to what it could be, he slowly started creeping toward where the noise was coming from. He couldn't imagine anyone else being out here. No one comes to see him, and no one else lives out this way. *Unless it was Pudgy coming out here to arrest him*, he thought to himself. But as he got nearer, the noise stopped. The woods became really quiet, like it was holding its breath. He kept walking closer to where he thought the noise had come from. He stopped momentarily to see if the noise resumed. He stood very still and tilted his head. With all the stillness, he thought he could hear his own heart beating. He started walking again.

Something didn't feel right, but he couldn't stop himself from trying to find the source of the noise he had heard. He could almost see his camper. As he came upon a thicket, he saw what he thought was rags. He kind of chuckled to himself thinking he had been afraid of someone dumping their trash. From time to time people did that. Disgusting as it may have been, he felt better. It wasn't something sinister, and he would do like he usually did and clean it up and take it to the dump. But as he started to reach down to the rags, he saw that it wasn't rags—it was clothing, and out of the clothing there was a hand sticking out. Fear gripped him, and he was about to run away when something hit him in the head from behind.

When Never came to, he slowly sat up and reached up to feel the big lump on the back of his head. There was no blood, probably because his hat had taken most of the impact. He looked around to see if anyone was still there that may have hit him. Not seeing anyone he got to his feet and ran as fast as an old man could to his camper. He was struggling to catch his breath by the time he reached for the camper door. He climbed in and paddle-locked his door, something he never did before. He took a seat in the nearby kitchen chair, still in his heavy coat, sweating. But not from being too warm. From fear. He couldn't help thinking someone may be dead and someone tried to kill him.

He decided he better either get out of town while he could or . . . what? What could he do? He decided to hide out until he could talk to Billie. She wanted to help him. She was the only one who believed in him. Well, Billie and Miss Rose. Maybe Suzy . . .

Finally, he stoked up his nerve and put on his coat. He turned the key in the paddle lock and opened it. He took a deep breath and slowly opened the makeshift door. He looked around but didn't see anyone. He quickly walked to his truck and got in. He headed to the Inn.

Tony and I were sitting in a booth at the Over Easy and waiting on our food.

"You're going to be sorry that you didn't order the cinnamon almond French toast" Tony said smiling as he leaned on the table and teepee'd his hands in front of him.

"Oh no, I'm not. I'm going to eat one of yours" I said and then sipped on my coffee.

"Ha ha, so you think."

I ended up ordering some of my own French toast. It was that good. Tony kept me laughing talking about our past escapades as children. He even mentioned something about my boogeyman in the closet. Boy, if he only knew. He tried to get me to tell him what spooked me into running into the Water's Edge like a nut. I objected to "nut," but I said I just had a lot on my mind. We had just finished up our breakfast when I casually broached the subject of his love life. Not really, I went head on.

"Who is she?"

"Who is who?"

"This mystery woman that you are seeing. That you are getting all pretty'd up and smelling good for? That you are sneaking out at night to see." He frowned at that comment.

"Now why would I have to sneak out to see anyone? And why would you care? I don't remember you consulting me about—"

"Don't say his name," I interrupted.

"I'll fess up to one thing. When your boyfriend was here last summer, I found his bottle of skin so soft that he was using to fight our mosquitoes. Yeah, I was lowlife'd and snuck into his stuff on a 'bathroom run,' and I dumped it out and put water in it. The mosquitoes were eating him alive." He started laughing, and then he said while cracking up, "And I'm not sorry." Then I joined him in laughing. And here I thought Pig Slop was just hitting himself all the time to be a jerk.

"Okay, but stop trying to avoid my question. Who is she? Let me decide what horrible thing I could do to her to make us even." I smiled but kind of meant it too.

"Billie, I . . ." Before he could say anything more, I saw him look past me. I turned to see what he was looking at. Sandy had just walked in. She looked around until her eyes found Tony. She unconsciously patted down her braids and switched her hips to where we were sitting. She never once looked at me, only Tony. Oh crap! It's Sandy! He is seeing her. Geesh!

"Hi, baby," she purred. It made my breakfast churn. Especially when I looked over at Tony and he was smiling at her. Before he could say anything, I butted in.

"Hi, Sandy. What have you been up to?" I cheerfully said and didn't care what she had been up to. I have never liked her, and I'm pretty sure the feeling was mutual although she tried really hard not to show it with her response.

"Save it, Billie." She looked at me with disgust. Then she flashed those hot-pink nails at me as if to say "Run along." Ha, I noticed one was broken. "Don't you have an Inn to run? Tony and I have some grown-up talking to do, don't we, Tony?" she cooed. I don't know why Sandy and I have never gotten along. She had always been on the snotty side when she talked to me, so I returned the tone with her. Visions of pulling out one braid at a time from her head were running through my mind. I looked at Tony, and he was still smiling at her, and that really got under my skin.

"Tony and I were just having our own grown-up talk, weren't we, Tony?" My voice matched her cooing one. "So maybe you might want to slither back under that rock you came out from." And then I batted my eyes and gave her a smile as fake as her nails with my mouth closed and then with teeth.

Sandy let loose with a string of cuss words that I didn't know you could put together like that. She had talent. I shook my head as if to clear some unseen hair, squinted my face into a mean mug, and confidently answered with a witty response. "Oh yeah?" Okay, it wasn't that witty, but it was all I could come up with. Then I used a few choice words and was holding my own. I guess Tony was over being amused and had enough. He tried to calm us down, and that just riled us up even more.

Martha was an older black woman, who was the second generation to own the Over Easy. Her son, Daryl, was the cook and would someday inherit the Over Easy from her. She had known all of us since we were babies. She came by the table and asked, "You all need anything?" I know she heard most of it, but to her credit, she smiled cheerfully at us and started taking away dirty dishes.

With that, Tony chuckled and replied. "A saucer of milk for two maybe." Martha laughed and walked away with our dirty dishes.

Finally, I had enough and fished the clean Sexy shirt out of my purse. Some change fell out on the table, and I stood up. I grabbed the change and stuffed it in my pocket. I said, "Tony, darling, I forgot to give you back the shirt I borrowed when I spent the night." I tossed it to him. "I still think it's a stupid shirt, but I did need to have one on to go home." And with that, I got up and walked out without turning around.

CHAPTER 27

Sandy fumed as Billie walked out. She was messing up her plans. "Is that true?" Sandy demanded.

"Every word," Tony responded. That was not what Sandy wanted to hear. She went back into a frenzy.

"Look, Sandy, I don't want to talk about Billie, and I really need to get back to the Water's Edge." Tony was still sitting in the booth. Although uninvited, Sandy had taken the empty spot across from him. He signaled Martha for the check.

"So are you just going to ignore me now?" Sandy said as Martha approached the table, halting the conversation.

"Here's your bill, Tony. Did you want something, Sandy?"

"Yes, but it's not on the menu." Tony took advantage of the interruption and stuffed some cash into Martha's hand.

"Gotta go! Thanks, Martha, for a great breakfast. See you around, Sandy." He bolted out of the restaurant leaving Sandy to stew.

"Yes, you will." She said as she watched Tony leave. Martha finished clearing the table and shook her head in disgust. *Young girls nowadays!* she thought.

I decided to take the route back to the Inn along the lakefront. I love our lake. Maybe it would calm me down. I was pretty mad. That Sandy! Oh god, it can't be her. What would he see in her? She isn't even likable. I got near the Water's Edge and was really fuming by then. I saw a rock and kicked it. Big mistake. My Converses didn't cushion any of the rock's blow to my big toe. I started jumping up and down on one foot, yelling, "Ow ow ow ow."

"You okay, Billie? That rock looks pretty vicious." I turned to see John, of course, sitting on his chair sneaking a smoke, smiling. I rolled my eyes and limped over to him. I took the chair on the other side of the small table. I sat down with a thud and blew out air.

"Oh, you're hilarious. And stop smoking." I reached over and pulled the cigarette from his hand, and in my best imitation of Betty Davis, I threw my head back gave my hair a shake and took a long drag and pretty much hacked up a lung. I stubbed it out into a mash of tobacco and paper.

John just smiled and calmly lit up another one. "So why are you mad at the rock?"

"Because it is stupid. Stupid, stupid, stupid, stupid. It doesn't know it's being stupid over a female rock with braids and false eyelashes and nails." I spat out "with braids and eyelashes and nails." John looked a bit puzzled but let me spew. I took off my shoe and rubbed my sore toe. "Well, if your brother thinks she's the one, then he deserves her." I saw John move his gaze from me to something behind me and then he smiled wider. "He's behind me, isn't he?" John quickly nodded his head. I blew out air. I got up and turned to Tony. I tapped him on his chest with my Converse in my hand. "Stupid," I yelled at him. And then with the little dignity I had left, holding my shoe, I hobbled off to the Inn. There was very little snow on the ground but enough to make me wince from the cold. But I didn't want to wait and hear if John and Tony were laughing at me.

John and Tony watched me limp away.

"You have her rattled," John said

"Man, every time we're together, we fight," Tony said as he sat down and pointed at John's cigarette. "Why are doing that to yourself?"

"I don't know. I just don't know." John took a drag and looked out at the lake thoughtfully. "You know, I wanted what Dad and Mom have and thought that was how our marriage was going to be." He turned and looked at his brother. "I didn't even make it a year. Should have thrown minute rice." He smiled as he said it. "I had plans. I wanted to add a full-blown restaurant to the Water's Edge. We have the land for it. A nice place that would attract people into the Village."

"So why don't you just do it? What's stopping you?"

"It was just a dream, I guess." He took a big drag and blew it out through his nose. "Women, can't live without them, can't make them stay."

"So, you're just going to smoke and drink yourself to death instead of finding the right woman? She wasn't the right one for you. I think you know that."

"Yeah, you're right. Maybe Billie's the right one." He smiled and took a drag of his cigarette. He blew a smoke ring.

"You're such a jerk." They both started laughing.

Inside, I yelled to Zeke that I was back. He floated down the steps dressed just like Tony had been dressed and asked, "So, how was breakfast?" He did that thing with his transparent eyebrows again. I see I'm going to have to cut him off the Hallmark channel. I threw my Converse at him, and it went right through him. It knocked a picture off the wall and the glass shattered. Just perfect.

After cleaning up the glass, I headed over to the Ivy House. Never and Suzy had the Ivy House looking wonderful. Never had done a wonderful job of cleaning up the yard. It was such a transformation from how it looked before. I figured I would have Never paint it in the summer, that is, if he wasn't locked up by then. I blew out air.

I had drawn a sign that said "Welcome to Your New Home" and taped it on the screen door. As I opened the screen door, the first thing I noticed is that it didn't groan as I pulled it open as it did before. Never must have put some oil on the hinges. I then opened the door, and my mouth dropped open. Gone was the old musty smell. Gone was the dust, grime, and drab environment that was once trapped inside. Instead, was a bright, cheerful, airy room that smelled of eucalyptus and lavender. As I inspected each room, I was pleasantly surprised at all the special accents that Suzy had strategically placed here and there. Along with all of Aunt Mae's and Uncle James's things, I had given her approval to use items that we no longer used at the Inn that was stored in the basement. She turned the Ivy House into a home. I was so thankful I almost cried.

About then, I heard a car door slam. I quickly went outside. Aunt Mae was helping Uncle James from the passenger side of the car. We all hugged, and I ushered them inside. Their eyes moved all over the beautiful little cottage that would be their home. I could tell they were pleased. We sat Uncle James in a chair and made him comfortable. I ordered gourmet hamburgers with exotic cheese and wine sauce for Aunt Mae and me and a chicken salad sandwich for Uncle James from the Water's Edge. He was probably going to look at it like Uncle Pete did his tuna sandwich, but he wasn't getting anything else. The food was going to be delivered. Aunt Mae and I walked around so that she could see all the things Never and Suzy had done. I could tell she was happy.

I heard a knock at the door, and there was John with a box. After hugging Aunt Mae and Uncle James, John acted as our waiter and served us all our food. John had made it extra special and added delicious sides and a large jug of raspberry lemonade. It was delicious. John had a talent for putting together the right ingredients and taking the ordinary and making it extraordinary. John insisted on cleaning up, and after he was done, he hugged it out with all of us and left. I left soon after that to give them alone time in their new place.

I decided to go out to Never's camper. While showing Suzy the stuff in the basement to use for the Ivy House, I found a nice lawn chair that we weren't using and wanted to replace the kitchen chair by his front plywood door. It even had cushions. I hoped he would like it. I had borrowed Uncle James's Yukon. The chair was so large it would never fit in my bug.

I pulled up in front of Never's camper, and it was just as dreary as it had been the last time I was there. I thought about how Suzy and Never had turned the Ivy House into a treasure and wondered if the same magic could happen here. Of course, it would take a lot more work, and I don't know how Never would feel about it. This was his home, and maybe this is how he wanted it. I didn't see Never's truck, but I knocked on his door to make sure. He wasn't home. I decided to just leave it. I thought or hoped it would be a pleasant surprise when he got home and saw the chair.

I pulled the chair frame out of the back of the car and carried it up to the front door. I carefully picked up the old chair and looked around for somewhere to put it. I shouldn't have drunk so much of that raspberry lemonade because now I had to pee. First things first. I decided to take the old chair around to the back of the camper. I was thinking about going back for the cushions when I really felt like I had to pee. Oh no. There was no way I was going to use Never's outhouse. Geesh! I didn't feel like I could hold it either. I decided to go behind the camper, but it felt so open that I was afraid someone, I don't know who, would see me. I kept walking until I started to get into a more wooded area. I kept walking and looking back to make sure I could keep the camper in my eyesight. I didn't want to get lost in the woods either. Deep in thought about where to pee, I decided on a spot. I pulled down my pants and some change I had in my pocket fell out. I could see it and quickly scooped it up dirt and all without looking at it. I put it all in my pocket. I really had to go. I squatted while holding on to a tree branch so that I didn't pee on my clothes. It was such a relief to finish that I almost missed seeing a hand sticking out of the dirt near where I just peed. Next to it was a bloodied-up wrench. I could just make out the words "Thank you for your hard work, Governor Jay Hammond."

CHAPTER 28

"Aaaaaaaaah! Oh my god, oh my god, oh my god, oh my god, oh my god, oh my god, oh my god, oh my god," I yelled. Then I tried to pull myself together. I looked around to see if there was any movement. Although I wasn't cold at all, my teeth were chattering. Maybe it was a mannequin's hand. Never collected all kinds of things. Yeah, silly me. I reached down and nope. "Aaaaaaaaah!" It wasn't a mannequin. I stood there screaming for a while before the thought came to me that maybe I wasn't alone out here. I looked all around for any sign of anyone. The sun was way on its descent, and it would be dark in another hour or so. I took a deep breath and pulled myself together again. I pulled my cell out of my pocket and called Pudgy. I told him what I found, and of course he had to become the Pudgy that he was back when I was six and saw Zeke for the first time.

"Come on, Billie. Did it come out of the closet and tap you on your shoulder?" Although I could tell he was eating something I could hear the sarcasm in his voice.

"Look, Pudgy, I have a very short time to hold myself together before flipping out completely, and the first person I'm coming for when that happens is you if you don't drop whatever it is you are chewing on and *get your big butt over here.*" I guess that got his attention because he went into Chief Pudgy mode and told me not to move or touch anything until the police got there. He didn't want me to contaminate the crime scene any more than I did. I wondered if I should tell him that my DNA was saturating the crime scene but decided I would keep that to myself. I could hear the sirens getting closer and car doors slamming. I yelled out so that they knew where I was. I could see them, but they couldn't see me to clearly, so I kept yelling.

"I see ya, Billie. Here we come." Pudgy directed the rest of the enforcement team in my direction. They carefully walked in a line so that they didn't trample the crime scene. As Pudgy got near, I pointed to the hand. A crime scene photographer started taking pictures, and Pudgy signaled for one of the officers to take me to one of the police cars. I got in the backseat and was instructed to wait with the officer who identified herself as Officer Janet O'Reilly.

I guess my teeth were chattering loud enough to be heard, so she got a blanket out of the trunk and wrapped me up in it. I could hear the police over the radio in the squad car. "Is there someone I can call for you?" She asked. I didn't want to scare my aunt and uncle. It was too far for my family to drive up, so I asked if she would call Tony. I gave her the number, and shortly after that, Tony arrived. Police had held him back until Officer O'Reilly yelled to them to let him through. She opened the door, and he hopped in. He took me in his arms, and I started to cry. He held me tight, and the tears just fell. He whispered, "It's okay, just let it go. I'm here."

It was dusk by the time the ME arrived. Soon after we watched the EMTs roll a gurney out of their truck. Then we watched them bring out the gurney with the remains covered in a white sheet and load it into the coroner's vehicle. Officer O'Reilly said that I was to go to the station in Baldwin to have my statement taken and that Uncle James's SUV would be brought over in the morning. Tony guided me to his Ranger, and we started up the road. He held my hand the entire drive over.

"I got you, Billie." He kept saying. I had such a lump in my throat I couldn't talk. I just let him keep reassuring me, and it made me feel a little better. We arrived at the station, and after my statement was taken, they let me leave with Tony.

As Never approached the Inn, he decided to hide his truck out in the woods in case he had to make a fast getaway. He hid his truck in someone's pole barn. He wasn't guilty of anything, but that didn't mean that anyone would believe him. He had lived out in the open world for so long he just couldn't imagine being locked up and for something he didn't do. And Jasper already had the law on him for a robbery he didn't do. Nope, he wasn't going to be locked up. He walked toward the Inn and peeked in the windows looking for Billie. There weren't any signs of anyone at home, but he knocked at the door anyway. No one answered. Then he tried the door, but it was locked. Not knowing what to do, he looked down at the boathouse. He thought he could hide out there until Billie came back.

Tony drove me back to the Inn. He took my keys and unlocked the door and walked me in. He sat me in front of the fireplace. He went to work on a fire, and by then John had come over. John went to the kitchen, and I could hear cabinet doors open and shut. I looked up and saw Zeke sitting on top of the floor lamp.

"What happened? You look awful."

"I'm fine," I said to Zeke.

"I know you are, baby. I just want to take some of the chill off you." Tony answered as he kept working on building a fire.

"I just found a dead person. At least I think it was a whole person. All I saw was a hand." Zeke looked shaken.

"It's okay. I'm so sorry. Is there anything you want or need?" Tony said.

"Who was it?" Zeke asked.

"I don't know who it was."

"Of course you don't. Don't worry about it. The police will figure it out. Does it help to talk about it, honey?" Tony wanted to know. He couldn't hear Zeke, and I had to answer without sounding crazy. Wait, he called me "honey." I smiled.

"That man Never was here earlier. He was looking for you. I saw him sneak out to the boathouse," Zeke said. "He looked bad."

"Really?" I said, and when Tony turned to look at me, I went on to say, "Yes really, it's okay. I mean, it was terrible, but I'm feeling better now." John came in with what looked like a cup of cocoa.

"Here ya go," he said. I timidly tested it for heat, and when I felt I could drink some, I did. It had whipped cream on top and was delicious. I felt myself warming up. I wanted to talk to Never but couldn't figure out how to do it with Tony and John here.

"Thanks, John." He looked down and gently wrapped the blanket around my legs and wiped the whipped cream off my nose with his finger. "I called your mom. Mom made me do it before you get mad." He smiled. "I also called Aunt Mae and promised her that me and Tony would take care of you. She needs to stay with your uncle. I will check on them tomorrow for you."

"Thanks, John, and thanks, Tony. I'm sorry I was such a jerk earlier. You both are the best friends I have." I was grateful for them both and felt a bit guilty for not letting them know about Never, but I'm pretty sure they would insist I call the police. I wasn't going to do that to Never.

"We love you, Billie," Tony said and sat down next to me and wrapped me up in his arms. I could see Zeke doing the eyebrow thing again.

"Okay, don't get all mushy. Hey, who's minding the Water's Edge?" I asked.

"Dad and Mom are. They insisted that we made sure you were okay. You've been going through a rough patch lately, and we wanted to make sure you didn't do anything crazy." John paused and then said, "Well, more crazy." He smiled.

"I'm fine. I just want to go to bed." I yawned. "You guys are the best, but really, I'm okay." Just then my cell rang Georgie's ringtone. Great! Just what I needed.

"I'm setting up a Zoom call. Look at the invite. It's coming through in a few minutes." Great. I love my family, but I really wanted to talk to Never.

"I'll go over and hop on at Aunt Mae's. Send me the link too, Georgie," John yelled.

"Thanks, John. Sending it now." He took my cup to the kitchen and came out a bit later with another one for me. "Take this one, Billie. I put more mocha on top." He handed one to Tony too. Then he left to go to Aunt Mae's.

We had our Zoom call, and everyone felt confident that I wasn't going to do anything rash. I kind of learned my lesson on that front. Zeke watched closely as we had our Zoom call, and I could see another lesson in technology coming. John and Tony said they would watch out for me, and that seemed to make everyone feel better. My family said they would come if I needed them, but I told them I was okay and just wanted to rest. I was getting so sleepy. It was getting hard to keep my eyes open. I dozed off during the call, and a little later, I felt myself being carried into my bedroom. I think I felt a sweet kiss on my lips, or maybe I dreamed it.

CHAPTER 29

I slept until morning. I slowly opened my eyes and stared at the ceiling. Yesterday's event came back to me like a snowball in the face. I wanted to believe it had been a bad dream, but when I looked down and saw that I had slept in my clothes, I knew that John had doped my hot chocolate and that Tony had put me to bed. I got up and quietly walked out of my bedroom. I listened to see if Tony was still there.

"Tony left about an hour ago," said Zeke, floating in the hallway. He had his old clothes on. "He didn't get much sleep, worrying about you."

"John put something in my cocoa, so it made me sleep. Where is Never?"

"Still in the boathouse."

"Okay, thanks. Have you seen any signs of other people hanging around?"

"I saw a couple of men dressed like this." And poof, he was in a policeman's uniform.

"They are looking for Never. I better take the tunnel." I threw on my coat and shoes and grabbed the flashlight. I headed down to the basement. This didn't feel as creepy as it did before. I went into Aunt Mae's canned goods room and worked the latch. Zeke oiled it good because it popped open without me having to pry it open. I hit the button, and as the secret door opened. I walked into the tunnel. When I got to the other side, I turned off my flashlight. I quietly opened the hatch door and climbed out into the secret room. I peeked through the opening that Zeke showed me, and yup, I could see the outline of Never even though it was very dark. I quietly hit the mechanism to open the door and crept out.

"Never? Never, it's me, Billie. I know you are here," I whispered. I turned on my flashlight and shined it on myself and then over at Never.

"How did you know I was here? How did you get in here?" He said as he looked around.

I avoided his questions. "There may be police out there, so we need to move out of here quickly without being seen. We have to go to the Inn a different way." I had already made up my mind that I had to let Never in on the secret tunnel. I wondered how many innocent people were saved by this tunnel. Well, I needed it to save one more. "Follow me and keep quiet." Like I needed to tell Never to keep quiet. I guided him to the back room, and Never obediently followed me without saying a word.

I led Never through the secret door, down the hatch, down the stairs, and through the tunnel. He never uttered a word. When we got to the other end of the tunnel, I told Never to stand back. I pushed the button, and the secret door opened. We walked into the back of Aunt Mae's canned goods room.

"Follow me," I said as I led him through the basement to the stairs. When we finally got to the kitchen, I told him to sit down at the table and then went to make sure all the doors were locked and the curtains and shades were pulled close. I didn't want any unwanted guests. I brought a blanket to put around him. I'm pretty sure it was cold in the boathouse last night. Zeke had turned on the little TV in the kitchen and put on a pot of coffee during the time I was out at the boathouse.

"I heard there were tunnels here but never found any," Never said.

"Please don't tell anyone about it, Never," I said. The coffee aroma permeated the kitchen. I got two cups down and poured Never some coffee. I looked over at Zeke, who was perched on the refrigerator and silently mouthed "Thank you." He gave me a head nod.

"I won't, Billie. Thank you." I was afraid he was going to get back to his earlier questions, but he didn't. I looked down at my empty cup and started to pour coffee into it when the local news came on. The body I found had been identified by her husband. It was Rachel. I looked at Never, and he hung his head. The TV was droning on in the background. He then looked up at me and sadly said, "That poor young lady. I know she had a hard life. I felt so sorry for her. Well, he can't hurt her anymore."

Then we heard the newswoman say, "Her husband said he thought his wife was visiting her mother. He didn't realize she hadn't made it to her mother's home in Kentucky. The police are trying to find the owner of the property where the body was found for questioning."

I reached up and turned off the TV. Never looked like he was in shock. I could see he had started shaking.

"I thought they were rags until I saw a hand. The last thing I remember was a flash of bright color. Someone hit me from behind. When I woke up, I ran and hid in my camper for a while before coming here. I guess I should have called the police, but no one is going to believe me," Never said sadly.

"I went out to your place, but you weren't there. You must have been in the boathouse by then. I found Rachel's body and called the police. I saw your wrench next to the, um, Rachel. It was covered with blood." Never's eyes grew wide, and his mouth dropped open.

"I don't know how my wrench got there. Last I saw it, it was in the back of my truck. It sure wasn't by Rachel, or I would have probably picked it up. I would never hurt anyone. I had no reason to harm Rachel." Never was really shaking now. He put his elbows on the table and put his head in his hands.

"Never, I hate to tell you this, but you need to go to the police station and turn yourself in. I will see what I can do to help you, but you are making yourself look guilty. Here, have some more coffee, and I will make you something to eat. Then we will go to the police station together."

I was concentrating on getting him some coffee when all of a sudden, he jumped up and almost knocked his chair over. He looked like he had seen a ghost. I cut my eyes over to where Zeke was hovering, and he was rapidly shaking his head as if to say "It wasn't me."

"What's wrong, Never?"

"Nothin'. I gotta go, Billie."

"But you didn't have anything to eat, and we were going to the station. Come on, sit back down, and have some breakfast with me."

"No. I gotta go." And with that he bolted out of the door. I stared at the empty doorway for a moment before turning my attention to Zeke.

"What did you do?"

"I didn't do nothin'."

"Do you think he could see you?" I asked as I reached up in the cabinet for a box of Honey Nut Cheerios. Now that Never wasn't going to have breakfast, I wasn't going to cook anything.

"He wasn't lookin' at me. He was lookin' out the window at somethin'." Zeke said as I pulled a bowl out of another cabinet. I pulled a spoon out of the dish rack. I glanced up at the window and although I had pulled the curtains there was a slight gap.

"What was he looking at?" I asked as I poured the cereal into my bowl. Zeke floated into the refrigerator and pushed the door open from the inside and carried the milk over to the table.

"I don't know. I was too busy lookin' at him. That poor man needs help."

"Well, something spooked him, and if it wasn't you, I don't know what it could have been." I was crunching on my cereal. Zeke looked at me a little upset. I think I had hurt his feelings about being a ghost. Lucky me, not only do I have a ghost, but a sensitive one at that. "Look, I am sorry, but you watched all the movies. People are normally afraid of ghosts. But let's get back to Never. Something sure spooked him."

"Who are you talking to?" Tony asked as he came through the backdoor.

"How did you get in? I locked all the doors," I asked. I put down my spoon. I know I locked all of them. "Don't you ever knock? I could be walking around here naked!" I ended up folding my arms in front of me.

"Really? Do you walk around here naked?" He did that eyebrow up-and-down. What is up with men doing that? "I think it would only be fair since you've seen my naked butt thanks to Mom." He smiled, and it was hard to stay indignant when he smiled. "You know Aunt Mae leaves a key"—he held it up—"under the flowerpot next to the door. And she told me and John that we never have to knock." I started to say something about the "new sheriff," but he stopped smiling and said, "I came back over to check on you. I thought you would still be sleeping. So," he said, looking around the room, "who were you talking to?" I stood up and put the milk away in the fridge. I started walking in the direction of the common room with Tony following close behind me.

"Just thinking out loud. Never just left. Before you say anything, I tried to talk him into going to the police. He was going to go but I guess changed his mind and ran out." I don't have much of a watch ghost. Everyone just pops in unannounced. I turned around and was facing Tony. "I'm okay, Tony."

"You scare me, Billie. I know you don't think he could be, but what if he is the murderer? You found the body. They just said on the news that it was Rachel Pennington. I came over to see if you were awake and tell you. Billie, you can't take chances like that. I'm spending the nights here until the murderer is caught."

"Oh no you're not." I fumed. "Just who do you think you are? I am my own person, and I will take care of me," I ranted. Tony pulled out his phone. "I don't need you or anyone else to protect me. I am not some weak female in some movie." He scrolled through his contacts and made a call. That was really ticking me off. He whistled as he waited. "Go home," I yelled. The Loving Arms landline rang. I held up my finger and ran into the office to answer it. He followed with his phone to his ear. "Get out," I mouthed. "Good morning, Loving Arms Inn. Billie Rivers speaking. How may I help you?" I said in my business voice ending with sticking my tongue out at Tony.

"Yes, hello. I would like to make a reservation." Tony mimicked my business voice. I blew out air and slammed the phone down. "Hey, is that any way to treat a customer?"

"Go home, Tony." I pushed past him and walked back into the common room. He followed. "You make me crazy."

"I had nothing to do with that." He smiled as he stuck his cell in his pants' pocket. Then he got serious again. "Look, Billie," he said, and I turned around to face him, "you are a woman here alone. Everyone in the Village knows that. There is a murderer on the loose and may have just left here. I would really feel better if you weren't by yourself. You have gone through a lot lately, and I worry about you." He paused for a minute and then said, "Would you consider staying with me instead?" I could see Zeke on the lamp doing his eyebrow thing. Geesh! All he needed was a cupid outfit and little hearts instead of eyeballs. I gave him a scowl, and then he disappeared. Good!

"And what would your Sexy-shirt girlfriend think of that? It's Sandy, isn't it?" I frowned and waited for the answer. Tony shook his head in frustration. "Don't tell me then. Look, I will be just fine. All the doors have locks, and apparently, I need to lock them and remove all of Aunt Mae's hidden keys," I said.

"Before everything went haywire, I thought the most we had to worry about was the Celebration party on Friday." He sucked in air and ran his hands through his hair. "Oh, man, we probably should postpone it."

"No, please don't. One thing doesn't have anything to do with the other. We all could use something to be happy about. What kind of 'surprise' are you doing?" Oh no, is he proposing to Sandy? He looked away and then started to say something. Suddenly, "A Ribbon in the Sky" by Stevie Wonder started to play. Tony looked surprised.

"Must be faulty wiring," I said through clenched teeth. "I'm going to have to get that fixed." And kill that matchmaking ghost.

"I wouldn't fix it." He gave me that priceless smile, and I could see a new thought crossed his mind. "Do you still dance?" He held out his hand. "Come on. Let's not fight. I only want you to be safe. Come on and dance with me and forget all about everything, even if it only lasts as long as this song." He paused for a second and said, "One more thing." He paused. "Let me lead." He still had his hand held out to me. It was making it hard to be mad at him. I took it, and he twirled me slowly around and then embraced me into a dance. Tony was a great dancer. Back in college he had done some ballroom dancing and been in competitions in Detroit. When I would come to the Village during our July stay, he would teach me. I could keep up with him but was never as good as he was at it. As he held me in his arms, I did start feeling tension leaving. He was warm and tender. He whispered in my ear, "Why do we fight all the time?"

"I don't know. Maybe we are both kind of stubborn," I whispered back. He pulled back and looked at me. "Okay, maybe I'm kind of stubborn," I said loudly. He smiled and pulled me close again. "I've been in a lot of messes lately. After the whole Pig Slop episode in my life, I just wanted a chance to figure things out on my own"—*and this whole Zeke thing*, I thought—"and then this happened, and I just want to have some space. Does that make sense, or am I going crazy?"

"No, baby, you are not crazy." He stepped back, still holding my hand. He took it in both hands and kissed it. He released me and backed away. "I'm just next door if you need me," he said and then walked out to the front door. I followed. Before going out, he dropped the key on the nearby table and hit the lock on the door.

I just stared as the door closed. That final click sound snapped me out of the fog. I blew out air and then yelled, "Zeke! Turn off that music!" It went *rrrrrp* and then silence.

CHAPTER 30

Rose was sitting in her living room watching the news. She had just poured herself a cup of coffee and was waiting for it to cool off before drinking it. Her sisters called and said they were on their way over. It was good because maybe it would take her mind off worrying about Never. *Oh, Never, where are you?* she thought to herself. Without thinking, she took a sip of her very hot coffee.

"Ow." She spilled a bit and pulled a napkin out of the holder and started wiping off her shirt. There was a knock on her door. Couldn't be her sisters already. Besides, they don't knock. She got up and pulled the curtain back to see who it was. She was surprised to see Pudgy at her door. She opened the door and told him to come in. He carefully wiped his feet on the rug before following her to the kitchen table.

"Is everything all right?" She pulled out a chair and sat down. She was worried that he was going to give her some bad news.

"Yes, Miss Rose. Everything is fine. I just wanted to ask you a couple of questions," he said as he removed his hat and took the seat across from her.

"Sure. Would you like some coffee?"

"No ma'am, but thank you. I know you probably know what has happened. A person can't fart in this Village without everyone knowing who did it." He chuckled until he saw the look on Rose's face. "Ah sorry, I mean to say that I'm sure you have heard about Rachel Pennington." He reached into his pocket and pulled out a small notepad. Since he could hear the news on her television in the other room, he went on. "What happened when Never came to the Pines and Needles after his argument with Jasper?" Rose didn't say anything at first. She didn't want to say something that would make Never sound guilty. "Miss Rose, I am just trying to get to the truth. Whatever it turns out to be." He reached over and patted her hand. She removed her hand. She told him everything except what Never said about making Jasper pay. Pudgy looked up from taking down notes and said, "There were other witnesses," he said.

"Then why are you asking me?" She could feel herself getting angry.

"Fair enough, fair enough. You sent Never over to the Cut Above to pick up a box for you." He was looking at a cardboard box that was on her counter that had a sticker on it that said "Cut Above Meats." He added to his notes. Without looking, she knew what he saw.

"Yes, but I told Never that I would go get it myself. I didn't want him to go anywhere near that crazy man."

"And did you go get it?"

"No, I guess Jasper delivered it himself." Pudgy just nodded like he was thinking to himself. "But I wasn't home when he delivered the box. He left it in my garage. He knows I have a refrigerator in there and has left things like that before when I wasn't home."

"Oh, so you didn't see Jasper when he delivered it?"

"No, in fact I was surprised when I went in the garage and saw the box." Pudgy was still nodding to himself and writing.

"Did you hear his truck? Did he knock at the door?"

"Look, Perry Mason, I told you I wasn't home. Daisy, Lily, and I went to pick up some material that was being held for me in Grand Rapids. We made a day of it. I didn't know he had even delivered the box until I went out to the garage later that night to get something out of that refrigerator." Pudgy put down his notepad and pen. "I don't know why he didn't call me and tell me he delivered it either. It's almost like he didn't want to let on what time he was here. Never is innocent and you know it." Rose leaned back in her chair. She was clearly mad.

Pudgy looked thoughtful. He picked up his notepad and pen and stuck them in his pocket. Then he rose to his feet. Rose got up too. As they walked to the door, he said, "If you think of anything else that may be of help, please contact me." He pulled on his hat as he stepped outside. He looked around and then turned to face her. "I know you want to help Never, but the only way to help is to be honest and—" Rose slammed the door in his face. He stood there for a minute before going to his squad car. She pulled the curtain to the side and watched him pull out of her driveway. Now she was really concerned about Never. Oh, she didn't think he was guilty of anything, but she remembered how it was during segregation and how innocent people end up in prison for life or worse for something that they didn't do. Never was already a broken man for some reason, and she was scared that this would break him beyond repair. Suddenly her backdoor swung open and in walked her sisters. She forgot that they were on their way. They were going on and on about what had happened. Rose started making more coffee. She had to think of what to do.

I decided that to help Never get this straightened out, I needed to go see Jasper. He was the best suspect, and well, I didn't like him. Anytime we went into the butcher shop, he always gave me the creeps. I don't know what it was about him. Maybe it was how he had a way of talking down to people. No, not just people. Black people. I got in my bug and drove over to his house. I saw his truck parked in the yard. I looked around and didn't see any of his neighbors out and thought maybe this wasn't a good idea. What if he did kill his wife? But how can I help Never if I don't find out who did it? I unbuckled my seatbelt and took a deep breath. I thought about leaving the car running but decided against it. I walked up to his front door and knocked. I didn't exactly know what I was going to say, but I figured I could make it up as I go. It worked for Jessica Fletcher on *Murder She Wrote.* The blinds on the door cracked open a bit, and then the door opened a crack. Jasper peeked out.

"What do you want?" he said.

"I just wanted to say I was sorry to hear about your wife. I'm the one who found her." The door was still barely open.

"What do want, a reward?" What a creep.

"Why, no. I just wanted to give my condolences. It must be terrible, and I am so sorry for your loss. I don't want to bother you, so I'll go."

I started to turn around when he said, "Wait." He opened the door and stepped back as he said, "Come on in." Geesh! This was as terrifying as going into Private or the tunnel that first time. I looked around and still didn't see any neighbors, but if I wanted to help Never, I was going to have to suck it up and go in.

To say it was dreary in that house would be an understatement. There was no feeling of love or no loss of love felt in that house. There were no family pictures on the walls or knickknacks or anything personal anywhere. It was a sad place.

"So, you're in here. What do you want?"

"I don't want anything. I feel just awful about Rachel, and I know you must feel even worse. I just wanted to tell you." I looked him dead in his eyes "I hope the police get the person responsible for Rachel's death." And I think he is sitting here with me.

"They'll find Never, and I hope they fry him. And all this time I thought my poor Rachel was at her mother's." He was looking around the room like he was figuring out what to sell the house for. He sure didn't look sad.

"And what reason would Never have to hurt Rachel? He didn't know her that well. None of us knew her that well."

"Are you crazy? For the money! He was after the money," he yelled. "There was five hundred thousand dollars in that register, and he got it." He looked almost defiant at me.

"How would Never even know about it? Did you tell him about the money? I don't think so. Did you tell anyone about the money? And where is the money? If Never ends up not having it, who does?" I saw him hesitate. He was hiding something.

"I think you better leave now, Billie. I'm still in mourning." Jasper said, trying to look sad. He stood up and started walking toward the door. Still in mourning. Ha. He sure didn't look like it.

I got up and said, "Again, I am very sorry for your loss." He opened the door, and I walked out. He slammed it shut. The venetian blinds on the door jangled.

"What in the world do you think you are doing, Billie?" Pudgy was standing in front of my bug leaning on it with his arms folded in front of him.

"Hi, Pudgy. I was just offering my condolences. There's no law against that, is there? Are you following me for some reason?" Out of the corner of my eye, I saw Jasper's blinds move. Pudgy saw it too.

Pudgy stood up, and it looked like my bug gave a sigh of relief. He walked over to me and quietly said, "This is a police matter. You need to stay out of it and let us complete our investigation." Then he looked me in the eyes, or at least I think he did. Couldn't tell through those dark sunglasses. He said, "Where is Never, Billie?"

"You still can't believe Never would do something like this. How would he even know about the money." I saw an eyebrow go up. Geesh! I shouldn't have said anything about the money. "There's something shady about Jasper."

"That may be, but he may have an alibi, and Never doesn't. Besides, if Jasper killed his wife, what do you think you are doing? Squeezing a confession out of him? And don't you think that would put you in a dangerous position? Keep out of it, Billie."

"What? And just what is this alibi?" I ignored all the stuff that made a lot of sense.

"Stay out of this, Billie." He turned and walked over to his squad car that was parked behind my bug and got in. He backed out and waited for me to get into my bug and drive off. I thought he was just making sure I didn't go back in, but as I drove off, I looked in my rearview mirror. I could see Pudgy driving back into Jasper's driveway.

CHAPTER 31

Two days passed and still no signs of Never. I guess living out in the wild made it easier for him to stay lost. He knew how to get food and where to get shelter. Every so often I would check in the boathouse and tunnel to see if he was there but didn't find him. I think he was too afraid to come to the Inn. Pudgy would check in with me periodically to see if Never showed up here. Everybody in town knows Never, and I hoped he found someone who was helping him. I wasn't so sure if he went to the police it would work out for him. I think with all the evidence that was stacked against him and him running only made him look guilty.

Zeke and I watched the news to see if there was anything new, and when Pudgy would stop by to "check on me," I would put on my Mrs. Baits hat and drill him for answers. Nothing new was all he would say. So I tried to just go through the motions of day-to-day living, but Never was always on my mind. Well, the laundry wasn't going to do itself, so I grabbed the basket of dirty clothes and carried it down to the basement. I set the basket down in front of the washer and started sorting my clothes. When I got to the pants that I had worn when I discovered Rachel's body, I heard change jingling. Oh, yeah, I forgot I put that change in my pocket. I emptied the contents into my hand and found along with that change was sand and something pink. I looked at that a bit closer. Ewwww. It was a piece of a hot-pink artificial fingernail. Either Sandy's or Tory's, I guess, but I couldn't figure out how it got in my pocket. I threw it in the trashcan with the sand. Something was rolling around in the back of my mind, but I couldn't bring it forward. I stood there staring but not seeing my pants in my hands. My mind then clicked over to Sandy. The thought that she could be whom Tony was seeing ticked me off all over again. I took it out on my pants as I balled them up with gusto and threw them in the washer with the rest of my clothes. I added detergent and softener. I slammed the lid close and started it up. I checked one more time in the tunnel and boathouse for Never. Not finding any trace of him, I went back upstairs.

Daisy and Lily left. Rose was almost afraid to watch the news because she thought at any time she would see where Never had been caught or worse, shot to death by the police. She paced the floor. She decided that she just couldn't stand by and watch the man she loved go through this alone. She put on her coat and grabbed the keys to the truck. Before she reached the door, she turned around and walked over to the hall closet. She opened it and sighed. She reached up on a shelf and pulled out a steel box. She unlocked it with the little key she carried on her keychain and opened it. She pulled out her husband's loaded pistol and stuck it in her coat pocket. She knew Never was innocent, but that left a killer on the loose. She got in her truck and burned rubber backing out of her driveway.

Never ran through the backwoods of the town. He knew every inch of the Village and felt he could keep out of sight. He had seen Jasper looking at him through Billie's window. It made his skin crawl and a chill run down his spine. All he could think to do was run. He didn't want Billie to end up like poor Rachel. She had been so nice to him. He left to keep her out of harm's way. He kept running, looking behind him to see if he was followed. He hid out for a few days in an abandoned ice house. No one had used it for many years. He tried not to think of food, but he was hungry.

He waited until it was dark and climbed out of the ice house. He headed for one of the summer cottages. Most people in the Village rarely locked their doors unless they were summer people. Summer people drained their pipes and turned off the electricity. They had a habit of hiding a key somewhere. Never felt around pots, decorative rocks and bird feeders until he found a key. He unlocked the door and then put the key back. It was dark, and he wasn't able to see very well. He felt his way to the kitchen and found some cans of what he hoped was food, but beggars can't be choosers, as the saying goes. He hoped it wasn't dog food. He took a few cans and then felt around until he found a hand can opener in a drawer. He opened one of the cans, and luck was with him. It was beans. He pulled a spoon out of the drawer and ate the cold beans out of the can. It wasn't the first time he ate cold beans out of a can. He gathered up the rest of the cans and stuck the spoon and the opener in his pocket. He thought about taking a blanket, but he couldn't do it. He wasn't a thief, and he felt really bad about taking the food, spoon, and opener. He made a promise to himself that he would return them and pay for the food once he got out of this trouble. That made him take a deep breath and sigh. Will he ever get out of this trouble? He locked up the house and headed back. He passed a woodpile that had a tarp over it and grabbed it. When he got back to the ice house, he emptied his pockets. He laid down and pulled the tarp over him, and after all he had gone through, he fell into an exhausted sleep.

Through the night it stormed. The little ice house had no floor, and water was getting inside. When Never woke up in the early dawn, he was drenched. He decided he needed to change his hiding place to a dryer one. The rain had stopped, and the sun came out. As Never emerged from the ice house, he marveled at what the rain woke up. He could see green on the trees, bushes, and ground. It was going to be a nice spring day. He shook himself from his thoughts and remembered he had to find some kind of shelter. He looked around before quickly walking in the direction of the chapel. He thought he could be safe there. As he threaded his way through the forest, he was always on watch for either the police or Jasper. He was more afraid of Jasper finding him than he was of the police.

His damp clothes were heavy. He had to stop to catch his breath. He was close to the back of the chapel. He tried to slow down his heavy breathing and looked around him. He didn't hear or see anyone, so he crept up the back steps and tried the door. Locked tight. He knew the windows didn't open, so there was no sense in trying them. He couldn't stay on the run for much longer and felt his mortality slipping away. Through the tiny window in the door, he could see inside the chapel. He crept back down the steps and stood against the wall.

He shook his head and snorted out a small laugh. It was kind of ironic. Miss Rose was always trying to get him to come to this church with her to save his immortal soul, and now here he was trying to get in to save his life. Miss Rose would see the humor in this. All of a sudden, he thought of her. Not as Miss Rose, but as Rose. He slid down the wall and sat on the cold ground. He remembered the first time he saw her with her husband. He thought she was the prettiest woman he had ever seen before. He loved the color of her skin, her smile that felt like sunshine just seeing it, and the texture of her hair. But above all, he loved the sound of her voice. He remembered walking past this very church years ago when he first moved back here. He heard the choir singing. But what took his breath away was when the soloist began to sing. He had never heard such a beautiful voice. He had to see who it belonged to and was he ever surprised when he peeked in the church window and saw that it was Rose. He was so awestruck that he hadn't realized that tears had formed in his eyes.

From then on, he had been a bit obsessed with her and would often walk past the church on Sundays on the chance that she was singing. There were times when he would come in and sit in the last pew. He wasn't a jerk; he understood she was married and never let his feelings known. Besides, he liked her husband too and would come over often to watch him build furniture. Sometimes Rose would be working on her quilts and would sing while she sewed. The two men would smile as they listened, both happy to have her in their lives.

But when his son died, he stopped thinking about anyone, even himself. He shook himself out of his rhetoric and found new purpose. He didn't feel safe out here in the open and decided he would seek temporary shelter in Rose's garage. He knew where she hid her spare keys. He would rest there until he could think of what to do. He was pretty sure Jasper killed his wife and was trying, and maybe succeeding, in pinning it on him. He got up on his feet and headed over to Rose's place. It wasn't that far from the church, and he was partially down her driveway when her truck came barreling out. He was right behind it when it screeched to a halt.

"Oh my goodness, Never, are you all right? I'm so sorry. Are you hurt?" said Rose as she climbed out of her truck. Worry was all over her face as she rushed over to his side. "Why, you're soaked."

He sunk down to the ground behind her truck. "Sorry Miss Rose, I . . . I . . ." Rose could see he was struggling, and it broke her heart. She slowly squatted down beside him. The pistol in her jacket pocket fell out and clattered to the ground.

"Good lord, woman, what are you doing with *that*?" Never suddenly snapped out of his fog. He picked up the gun, opened it, and saw that it was loaded. He snapped it shut and handed it back to her. She started to put it in her pocket, but since it fell out, she just held on to it.

"I was looking for you. I want to help and protect you." Rose said.

His face softened. "You dear woman. I am in so much trouble I can't involve you—"

"We need to get inside, Never, and get you out of those wet clothes," she said as they both got to their feet. "If I have to encourage you at gunpoint I will, but I am going to make sure you are safe. And this is probably the dumbest time to say this." She hesitated and then went on, "I've gone this far I may as well go the rest of the way. I love you, you old fool." He smiled at her. He walked with her to her backdoor and turned her around to face him.

"Rose, I have been an old fool for too many years and let life pass by. But not any longer. Shoot me if you must, but I have a killer and the police on my heels, and I can't let anything happen to you. I'm going to turn myself in. It may be a long time before this all gets straightened out, but I will come back so that we can continue this conversation."

"I'm coming with you," Rose said stubbornly.

"You can't go with me. It's too dangerous. I promise you I'm turning myself in. Will you please trust me? I know I don't deserve your trust but just this one time. Now give me the gun and the keys to your truck." Rose hesitated. "I don't want you to shoot yourself." Rose saw the transformation of the old Never to this new one. She obediently handed him the gun. He stuck the gun in his pocket. She fished the keys out of her pocket and handed them to him. He pulled her to him and gently kissed her. When he stepped back, she still had her eyes closed and hadn't moved. He smiled and cleared his throat. She opened her eyes and stepped back. "I'll be back," he said.

"You better, or I'll come looking for you," she said smiling. She turned and headed to her backdoor. He watched her go into her house and then walked around to the driver's side of the truck. He opened the door and started to get in the truck when Jasper came out of nowhere and socked him a good one. He tried to hold on, but darkness came.

CHAPTER 32

It was Friday, the day of the Celebration, but it didn't seem like there was much to celebrate. I was still thinking about what to do about Never when Pudgy made one of his visits. We were sitting in the common room. Zeke was perched on the lamp.

"I told you, Never was here a few days ago, but he left. I don't know where he is now. Something scared him and he took off." I looked up at Zeke, who rolled his eyes. "I don't know where he went," I explained to Pudgy.

"He ran away because maybe he is guilty of something." He then dropped his official stance and said, "Look, Billie, I don't really believe Never would do something like this either, but as long as he is out there, he looks guilty, and that is what people are going to think."

"But he wouldn't do that. He isn't a thief or a murderer. Jasper could be both. He is despicable."

"So aren't you jumping to a conclusion of a man's guilt without investigation? If Never is innocent or Jasper is guilty, it is up to the law to decide, not you."

I ignored him and said, "Never told me he was hit over the head with something after he found Rachel. He didn't even know it was her because like me, all he saw was her hand. He didn't even see his wrench when he first saw her body, and it wasn't there when he came to. And why would he kill Rachel with his own wrench, leave her body behind his home, and leave the murder weapon beside her body? You have to be pretty stupid, don't you think? Never may be eccentric, but he is not stupid in any way."

"Then why didn't he call the police when he found her?" I could tell this was getting hard for Pudgy. He usually only had to handle people

---

who partied too hard or speeders. Not murder. I almost felt sorry for him. Almost. "If Never shows up here again, call me. Don't wait, call me. Never is in serious trouble. There are a few ways to look at this. What if he did do it? He could be dangerous." I started to interrupt, but he said, "Ah, that is what people are going to think because he has disappeared. He isn't safe running around on the loose." Now I was afraid that someone would shoot Never on sight. "Billie?"

"Yes, I hear you. I will call you if he shows up." I had my fingers crossed behind my back. I don't know why that was necessary when one tells a lie, but I wasn't going to buck that system. This was too important. Pudgy left and I turned to Zeke. "I've got to find Never and bring him back here. He may know more than what he said." About then, I heard the dryer buzz. With no one in the Inn, you could hear a fly sneeze. I got up and went downstairs to get my clothes out of the dryer. As I pulled each item out and put them in the basket, I got to the pants that I had on when I found Rachel. Something was still bothering me in the back of my mind.

I stared at the pants and then suddenly it hit me. I dropped the pants and grabbed the trash can. I ran upstairs where the light was better and carefully dumped the trash out on the top of the kitchen counter. I picked through as Zeke watched from the top of the fridge.

"What are you searching for?" he asked.

"Nothing now," I said as I just found what I was looking for. I stuck it and some change in my pants' pocket. "I'll be back. If Never comes back while I'm gone, lock him in until I get back." Zeke suddenly went *poof* and changed into Pudgy's uniform.

"No problem, Billie," he said. I blew out air. Geesh!

I ran across the street and walked into the Bait Shop. I saw Mrs. Baits.

"Good morning, Mrs. Baits."

"Good morning, Billie. Are you all right? I heard that it was you who found the body of that poor Rachel. What did she look like? How did you find her? Could you see blood? I bet it was terrible."

"Yes, ma'am. It was awful. I heard that you were there when Jasper threw Never out." I decided to turn the interrogation around and tell her nothing.

"You should have seen Never's face. He was embarrassed and mad at the same time. That awful Jasper threw him out the door, and poor Never almost knocked me down falling. I am sure that Jasper just hit Rachel because she had been yelling and crying for him to listen to her, and then all of a sudden, nothing. When I went in, she was rubbing her cheek. Said she fell." About then, Pudgy walked into the store. No one said anything. Even through his reflective sunglasses, I could see his face tightened a bit when he saw me.

"Hi, chief," I wiggled my fingers and said with a smile. He ignored me.

"I just wanted to make sure you didn't think of anything else," he said to Mrs. Baits. He and Mrs. Baits talked while I listened, but didn't find out anything more that would help. Then down one of the aisles I could hear, "You, you, you, Pig Slop . . .," and then Sandy laughing. I really couldn't stand her.

"Sandy, it's about time you showed up to work. Put down that phone and come up here to the register while I talk to Lewis," yelled Mrs. Baits. Pudgy had been one of Mrs. Baits's students too. This was just perfect. As Sandy passed me, I stuck out my tongue. Immature, I agree, but I felt better. I watched Sandy walk up to the counter, and she and Mrs. Baits exchanged spots. Mrs. Baits moved away from the counter, and Pudgy followed. I moved to the next aisle over from them so that I could hear what they were talking about.

"You don't really think that Never did this, do you?" Mrs. Baits said to Pudgy.

"Like I told Billie over there on the other side of this aisle, it isn't up to me to decide." Geesh! I'm not very good at covert situations.

I hurriedly picked up a few things and took them up to the front of the store. I laid them on the counter. I waited for Sandy to total it up. I held my breath. I was hoping it would come up an odd cent. If not, I was going to have to pick up something random until it was.

"That will be $10.41," Sandy said as she rolled her eyes. I smiled. I pulled a ten out of my wallet and made a big deal out of looking for some change. I pretended to look for change in my purse. I came up with a quarter. Then I acted like I just remembered I had change in my pocket.

"I forgot, duh! I have some change in my pocket." I pulled out the contents of my pocket and dropped it on the counter. If I wasn't wrong, this should spark something. I made sure Sandy looked as I found the correct change and handed it to her. I then I scooped everything else up and put it back in my pocket. She just glared at me. I could see the gears in motion in her head. About then Pudgy and Mrs. Baits walked up.

"Let me know if you think of anything else."

"Yes, so that he can pin it on Never." I couldn't resist saying. Pudgy gave me the follow-me signal, and we went down one of the aisles.

"Billie, I know you found the body, and I know how you feel about Never, but you saw his wrench. It was right there."

"His wrench was there?" Mrs. Baits had followed us down the aisle. Pudgy scowled at her. "This is my store, and I can go anywhere I want in it," she said indignantly.

"Now Mrs. Baits, don't you go telling people about that. I wasn't supposed to say anything about that. Darn it, Billie."

"Pudgy, wouldn't Jasper be a good suspect? Didn't Mrs. Baits tell you he hit Rachel?" I was stalling. I could still be wrong.

"She didn't see him do it," Pudgy said.

"And didn't he lie and say she went to see her mother?" I thought I had everything worked out except the motive. Besides, Pudgy didn't believe me in the past, so why would he believe me now? No, I had to prove who it was.

"Billie, stay out of it." And with that, he went out the door. The little bell over the door was the only thing that broke the silence.

"He's gotten too big for his britches, both figuratively and literally," Mrs. Baits said and kind of laughed. "I used to change those britches, too, so I know." Ewww. I could never unsee that. "So, Billie, what did you see when you found the body?" Uh-oh. Here comes the interrogation. I pretended to suddenly get a call on my cell.

"Hi, yes, I am on my way. I just stopped to pick up a few things." I picked up my bags, and Sandy gave me a mean mug look as I headed toward the door. Unfortunately, my cell started playing "No Scrubs" and blew my cover. I almost dropped my phone. That darn Pig Slop. I gave them a weak smile and ran out. I went back to the Inn to find that Pudgy and his merry men were there looking for Never.

"This time I do have a warrant." He tipped his hat up and scratched his head.

"You're wasting your time." I knew who it was, but I didn't know why or how to prove it.

Sandy shook her head. She watched Pudgy and Billie leave and scowled. Billie needs to mind her own business. Sandy headed to the back of the store and pulled her cell out of her pocket. She started to send a text when her attention went to a noise coming from the storage room. She walked back there and found Suzy.

"Why you hiding?" Sandy asked.

"I'm not hiding. It's called working, but you wouldn't know anything about that now, would you?"

"Why you smart—"

"Hey, you two, cut that out," Mrs. Baits cut her off before she could finish. "The bread man just got here, and I need someone to put it on the shelf before we close for the day. Why he came so late I don't know."

Suzy rushed past Sandy and started putting the bread away. Sandy leaned up against the wall thoughtfully. Why did Suzy hide when Pudgy came in? She was hiding something. Very interesting.

CHAPTER 33

I was told to sit on the porch and wait until they were sure Never wasn't there. They weren't going to take any chances with a suspected murderer. Zeke came out on the porch with me.

"Go listen to what they say." He nodded his head and floated off. After a while they finished. Of course, they found nothing and left. I looked at the mess they made and shook my head. "What did they say?"

"They really think he did it. The man you call Pudgy is going to be watchin' the Inn to see if Never comes back. One of them is supposed to follow you wherever you go. They have been searchin' the woods too but so far haven't found him."

"Hmmm. I suppose they have the back guarded too. Good." I reached down and opened the secret compartment on the desk and dropped the object from my pocket in there. "I think I know who killed Rachel, but I have no idea why. So I still could be wrong. It's good the Inn is under surveillance." Despite that, I was still scared that I may be confronting a killer. My stomach was dancing around like crazy. I was getting ready to call Pudgy to tell him my theory when suddenly I heard someone come in. I quickly ducked behind the desk.

"Billie, are you all right? What are you doing back there?" Aunt Mae was peering over at me behind the desk.

"Aunt Mae? What are you doing here?" I got up and brushed off my clothes. Aunt Mae looked at me with a worried look on her face. "I thought I saw a spider," I said lamely.

"Tony called me and told me he was worried about you being alone here. That got me worrying too." I pursed my lips together. So he sic'd Aunt Mae on me, did he. If I live through this, he is going to pay.

153

"Tony is so sweet," I said through pressed lips, "but he is worrying you over nothing. I only found Rachel. No one would have any reason to come looking for me. The police just searched the Inn, so I know I am safe here." I reached up and felt my nose to see if it was growing. "You have to go. Now." I rushed her out the front door. "Listen, Aunt Mae, I sent Suzy over to talk to you about helping you out at the Ivy House. She really needs the money, poor thing, and I just saw her, and she said she was on her way over. I don't want you to miss her because she's on foot. I would hate for her to walk all the way over and then all the way back without seeing her." I was rushing her along out to her car. I was sure I was going to pay for all the lies I was telling Aunt Mae, but I couldn't have her here in harm's way. I didn't want to be here in harm's way, but if my theory was right, there could be a murderer arriving soon.

"Okay. You are acting kind of weird, Billie. Are you sure you're okay?"

"Yes, ma'am. I was just going to lay down and take a nap. I didn't sleep well last night." More lies. I could feel Momma's Avon brush from times past. I looked down to see if my pants were on fire.

"Oh you poor thing. I'm sure you are just worn out from this terrible thing. Poor Jake, this has to be horrible for him. I sure hope he is all right. Well, if you need me, just call me. What did you say Suzy was coming over for?" Geesh!

"She thought she could come and help you take care of the housekeeping so that you would be free to take care of Uncle James." I'm sure Satan was brushing off a seat for me.

"Oh, that nice girl. Okay, I guess I better run." She climbed in the car and started it up. She rolled down the window and said, "You call me if you need me. Don't forget about tonight at the Water's Edge. I think it would be good for your Uncle James to be around a lot of his friends, but we aren't going to stay long."

"Oh, I forgot about that. See you there." I waved as she drove off and tried to look around to see if Zeke was right about the Inn being watched. I didn't want to set myself up to be killed trying to catch the killer. I could be wrong. I caught a glimpse of Pudgy; he wasn't very good at blending in. If there wasn't a killer coming to the Inn, it would have almost been comical. The killer had no idea that the Inn was under surveillance. Hopefully they couldn't see Pudgy.

I went inside and was standing in the common room. Maybe I should tell Pudgy. Geesh! I pulled my cell out of my pocket and before I could dial, my ringtone played "No Scrubs." Why does he keep calling? I guess I am going to have to block him. Like I didn't have enough going on. I swiped Ignore. Zeke, still in black-and-white sheriff clothes, appeared.

"You couldn't have warned me about Aunt Mae coming? I nearly wet myself."

"I didn't see her as a threat. She's such a nice lady." I don't think he understood my fear. If my hunch is right, I may be facing death myself. Oh boy, I just scared myself. Suddenly Sheriff Zeke disappeared and then reappeared. "There is someone sneaking around the backdoor. It isn't anyone I know. It may be safer to go to Private."

"Good suggestion." I quietly went up the stairs and into Private. I left it open a crack and listened. I turned around, and Zeke was right behind me. Oh boy. "Zeke," I whispered, "you don't have to hide here with me. Go see what is going on."

"Oh, right." He kind of laughed and disappeared. I didn't dare turn on the flashlight that I put next to the opening of Private, so my skin was crawling from both a possible killer in the house and being alone in the dark in Private. If I live through this, I am going to have to go to therapy. I put my own hands over my mouth so that when Zeke returned suddenly, I wouldn't scream. When he returned I was able to muffle my scream.

"It's some pretty colored lady. She is poking around looking everywhere."

"Where is she?" I asked.

"In the common room."

"Okay, it's showtime," I said as I creeped out of Private and started down the steps. I made a lot of noise coming down and hoped it was convincing. I turned and went into the common room. I made a jumpy motion when I saw Sandy sitting on the sofa. "Sandy, what are you doing here?

"I just came over to tell you that the police found Never. You seemed so concerned about that old bum I just thought you would want to know that." She smiled and it creeped me out. "Didn't you hear me calling you when I first came in?"

"No." *Because you didn't*, I thought to myself. "I was in the attic. You can't hear much up there."

"This is the first time I've been in here. I always wondered what it looked like. It's actually very nice." The way she said the word "nice" didn't sound like it was nice.

Right then my phone started playing "No Scrubs," and that is when

Sandy yelled, "Put that down." I looked up and took a deep gulp. Sandy was standing there pointing a very large gun at me. "Put it down, now."

I dropped my phone and hoped it didn't break. Sandy never took her aim off me and picked it up. She put it on the table next to her. "What are you doing? I know we aren't the best of friends, but what are you doing?" I tried to act like I hadn't figured it out.

"Shut up. Don't play that innocent game with me. I'm not stupid. I saw what you had, and I know you figured it out."

"What are you talking about?" I had to stall. I thought I would have had a chance if Pudgy would have come over to see why Sandy was here, but if he has Never, he was probably gone. I had a plan B, but it was a longer shot.

"*Shut up!* Boy, you just don't know when to shut up." I also could see Zeke next to Sandy. He had his Rocky boxing stuff on and began swinging punches that Muhammad Ali would have been proud of, but although he floated like a butterfly, his sting wasn't affecting Sandy at all. They went right through her. She didn't even flinch, so I'm sure she didn't feel anything. I better work on plan B.

"I think it would be best if you called for help. I'm sure this is all a misunderstanding." I was looking directly at Zeke when I said "you." After all my technology lessons I had hoped that Zeke paid attention to that one.

"Why would I call for help? Looks like to me you are the one who needs it. You must be touched in the head. No, don't you think about it." I had started to move toward her. It was enough of a distraction that Zeke was able to get my phone undetected.

"Why don't you put that down and let's talk." I could see my cell phone floating out of the room. From where Sandy was standing, she couldn't. Then I could see it being carried with my cell phone glove and then float back on the table next to Sandy. I decided to take a chance that Zeke figured out how to call. "Maybe you ought to tell me why you have a gun pointed at me, Sandy."

"Oh shut up. You know why, so stop acting so dumb." She changed the gun into the other hand and wiped sweat off her empty hand on her pants. "You just had to be everywhere. Why didn't you just butt out?" Her hand shook a little, and I was wondering if the cavalry was going to make it in time. This wasn't my favorite shirt, but I sure didn't want to mess it up with any bullet holes.

"Why did you kill Rachel?" I asked, trying to think of something to do before Sandy panicked and pulled the trigger.

"Yeah, why did you kill my wife?" Oh boy, we have another lowlife added to our gathering. Jasper, looking all sweaty and mean, just stepped in.

CHAPTER 34

"Jasper, quick, grab Sandy and help me," I yelled.

He just looked at me and said, "Why would I do that?" Then he looked at Sandy and said, "I told you Rachel was leaving me."

"You idiot. I didn't want her to take our money. Why didn't you tell me that you were going to take the money?"

"Why didn't you? I robbed my own store to be with you." Aha. I didn't think Tony would ever. *Okay, Billie, focus, get back to this life-and-death situation.* Oh no, those two were together? Now it all fits. "I knew I shouldn't have told you about the money."

"You should have told me. I had this all worked out," she whined.

"You stole Never's wrench out of his truck, didn't you?" I said, trying to get them back on point.

"Yeah, that stupid wrench that he shows everybody, and then I broke into the back of the store. I had on gloves. I watch all those crime shows." She looked at me for some weird validation. I nodded my head. "I was just about to break into the register when Rachel came in. I hid, and when she opened the register, I hit her with the wrench. Just to knock her out, but she wasn't moving. I thought I killed her. I guess I panicked. I dragged her out to my car and dumped her body in the trunk. This dead town closes up at six on Sundays, so no one saw me. I figured everyone thought she had gone to see her mother, so by the time they found out she wasn't at her mother's, we would be gone." She looked over at Jasper. "They would just assume she ran off. Her car is at the bottom of Mosquito Lake. But then Miss Busybody over there found her body. Glad I put that wrench with it." She smiled, thinking she was so smart.

"You idiot. I already took the money from the register. I was going to pin it on Never too. I didn't know he had touched Rachel's locket. Boy, was that a good fortune. I really thought Rachel had gone to her mother's, and all the time you had killed her? Boy, what a dumb move." He laughed, and then when she gave him the stink eye, he stopped. "I threw the burner phone into the lake, so you can't call or text me. I was scared the police would find it." Sandy just rolled her eyes.

"It was an accident, Sandy. You could still turn yourself in." I said, still wondering where the heck were my rescuers.

"You are so stupid. I should just shoot you now and be done with it." That shut me up. She looked back at Jasper. "Where did you put Never?"

"He's tied up in the meat cooler at the store. Guess now you are glad I staked out Rose Anderson's place. Rose, being a churchwoman and all, will have to swear in court that Never took her gun from her." Oh boy, now I know where Sandy's gun had come from. I started to see a neat little cleanup of loose ends, and I wasn't going to like the outcome.

"How could you let Never rot in prison for something he didn't do?" I had to keep them talking. I caught movement in the outer room. It was either help or another member of the nightmare Olympics.

"Someone has to go down, and it ain't going to be me or Sandy. Yeah, I wanted out of this stinking place as much as she did." He directed his gaze on Sandy. "No one would have put the two of us together. Ha, if my daddy knew about me and Sandy, he would kill me. Me and Sandy have been lovers since she was in high school. But I did a dumb thing and knocked up Rachel." He stole a glance over at Sandy, and she gave him the stink eye. "Her old lady was going to have me locked up for rape, so I said I would marry her. I had to wait until enough time had passed on running the butcher shop according to the stuff in my uncle's will, and then I was going to sell it, and me and Sandy were going to blow this town. But then I learned that Rachel had inherited all that money. That was my money! Money she paid for me to be her husband." I felt really sorry for Rachel. She didn't deserve the cards she had been dealt.

I looked over at Sandy and said, "So what happened? You said you thought you had killed her. You only stunned Rachel, didn't you? She wasn't dead."

"I drove out to Never's and dumped her next to his trailer. Thanks to old lady Baits, everyone in town knew about Jasper and Never's argument. Then I went and moved my car out of sight. I found an old sheet in some of Never's junk and put her in it and dragged her out to the woods. The ground was so hard I didn't leave tracks. I tried to dig a hole. The ground was like a rock, and I wasn't getting very far, so I decided to just cover her up with the sheet and leave her there. I figured they would blame Never for her death if they ever found her body. Then Never showed up. I barely got hidden. He saw her, and I couldn't have him blabbing about it until we had a chance to get the money and then get out of town, so I hit him with the shovel. I went back to digging thinking I would just kill him too and bury them both somehow. But when Rachel woke up, she started fighting me."

"That's when you broke your nail. During the fight." I had to keep her talking.

"I guess. I panicked and hid out in the woods until I could think. Then Never woke up and went into his camper. I waited a while thinking he was going to call the cops. Then he came running out and got in his truck and left. I put on my gloves and left the wrench next to her. As I was driving home, I passed you and Tony walking to the Over Easy. I hurried home and changed my clothes. I decided to go find Tony to sleep my way into an alibi. Everyone would think me and Tony were kicking it and have no idea about me and you." She looked at Jasper.

"Say what?" both Jasper and I said at the same time.

"Oh shut up. I could have talked him into giving me an alibi if I needed it. I'm sure he would have done that for me." I don't know which of us was getting madder at Sandy, but she was oblivious to it. "Pudgy and his dumb fat behind was sure it was Never who robbed the store. Who would believe anything that ratty old man told them, and nobody would connect me to you," she said, looking at Jasper. "I thought I was home free. It was funny because you really thought Rachel was at her mother's." She looked mad at me again. "But then *you* were with Tony, and then *you* found Rachel, and *you were everywhere*. I wasn't so sure then. The kicker was when you were in the store. I couldn't believe you pulled my nail out of your pocket."

"Up until then, I thought you killed your wife," I said, looking over at Jasper, trying to stall for time, "and the more you talked, the guiltier you looked. Well, you and Never." Then I looked back at Sandy. "When Never told me that he had seen a flash of bright color before he was hit with the shovel, it got me thinking. I remembered that you had hot pink acrylic nails that day in the Over Easy. You kept clicking them. But I noticed one of them was broken."

"I didn't realize I had broken my nail until later. I started to go back when I saw all the squad cars going out that way. I figured someone had found Rachel. I thought I had a stroke of luck when you had it, and it wasn't found by the police. I want it back. Now! When we leave here, I don't want to have to look over my shoulder. Where is it?" I gave her my best mean mug.

"I'll never tell where it is. *Never!*" She cocked the gun and aimed it at me. "I put it in a secret compartment in the desk." I popped it open so that she could see it was there.

"Get it."

"Get it yourself, you plan on killing me anyway." I sounded a lot braver than I felt.

"Yeah, but what to do with your body. Jasper, you're a butcher. You could cut her up and mix her in with the hamburger." Oh, I really didn't want to be on someone's dinner plate.

"Look, I don't want no murder rap. Sure, I took the money and I can't say that I am sad that Rachel is dead, but I'm no murderer." Jasper is such an upright citizen.

They argued for a minute about it, and then Sandy said, "Jasper, either you are with me or with her." She cocked her head in my direction. "Make up your mind." Just for effect, she aimed the gun at him for a moment before she turned it back on me. That's when I was sure I saw a bit of a shadow move in the hall. Then I saw a kind of puzzling sight. It looked like a faceless man in a hat and suit coming toward the doorway. About then Sandy saw it too and started shooting off her gun. I guess Jasper thought she was shooting at him, and he took off running. Through all the heavy smell of gunpowder and noise and distraction, I saw my chance to lunge at Sandy. I knocked her down to the floor. We wrestled over the gun, and luckily it wasn't pointed in any direction where it could do damage.

The "person" at the door disappeared, and I could hear someone running in the hall as I wrestled with Sandy. I grabbed some of her extensions and pulled them right out. That made her drop the gun. That was all I needed. I pulled her up by her shirt and socked her a good one in the jaw. She went down like Apollo Creed, and I could almost hear the Rocky music playing in my head. Zeke isn't the only boxer at the Inn. Still holding Sandy's braids, I lay on the floor, took a deep breath, and blew it out.

By this time, Pudgy had cautiously come in with his gun drawn. Tony and John were behind him.

"You can holster your weapon. I have the situation handled," I said from the floor. I heard that on TV many times and always wanted to say it. Pudgy put his gun away, and Tony pushed past him. He rushed over to me kicking the gun out of the way and started looking me over for bullet holes. "Are you okay?"

"Sorry, I knocked out your killer girlfriend." He smiled down at me. I looked at the braids in my hand and dropped them in disgust. "Ewww." About then, more policemen came in with guns drawn who had probably been hiding around the Inn, in hopes of catching Never. Pudgy called them off.

In all that chaos around us, Tony said to me, "There has never been anything between me and Sandy. Anything at all. I would think you of all people would know that. You crazy girl." I smiled. He hugged me and kissed me full on the mouth, and I kissed him back and wow! Wow, wow, wow, and wow. Suddenly I forgot all about everything except Tony's kiss. Then it really hit me. I love Tony. I have for a long time and had resisted the thought of it. Yes, this kiss was that long to have this epiphany happen. I heard Sandy stir, and she must have seen us kissing because I heard her say, "Oh———!" She has a potty mouth.

Pudgy cleared his throat and said, "Ah, sorry to break this up, but we have a murder to process." We broke away from the kiss, and Tony helped me get to my feet. "I'm glad you didn't say 'Ewww' and run away like the first time I kissed you," he said.

"Well, you have improved greatly since then," I said with a smile. I then said to Pudgy. "Not that you will need it, but here is Sandy's fingernail that was at the murder scene." I reached into the secret panel, which wasn't really secret now that all these people were standing around. "I accidentally scooped it up with my change and didn't know I had it until recently." Pudgy gave me a look. "Sorry."

Tony put his arm around me and squeezed. We could hear sirens in the distance getting closer. I happened to look up and saw Zeke perched up on a cabinet. He had a huge smile and gave me the up-and-down eyebrow move. I eyebrowed him in return and smiled. Tony must have thought I had taken a hit to the head. He looked in the direction that I was looking and of course saw nothing.

"Are you all right?" He was holding me so close I could feel his heart rapidly beating, or maybe that was mine. "Why did you take a chance like that? You could have been killed. When I heard those gunshots, I thought . . ." That is when it all hit me. I fought an armed psycho murderer and her booty call. Once again, I passed out in Tony's arms, but this time without the Jack Daniel's, puke, or Pine-Sol.

CHAPTER 35

All's well that ends well, as the saying goes. Zeke was the real unsung hero. He was able to call Tony, and Tony heard enough of the conversation with the gruesome twosome to get John to call Pudgy while he stayed on the line and recorded everything. Pudgy had been in his car parked in the Bait Shop and came running. He saw when Sandy walked in but didn't think anything was wrong. When one of his officers said they saw Jasper come in, he got curious but held back. They were waiting for Never. But when he got John's call and then Sandy started shooting, he came running with John and Tony right behind him. John had tackled Jasper to the ground as he ran out of the door. Pudgy's men had come out of their hiding places and took over for John. Pudgy and Tony crept in, afraid of what they might find. They came in just in time to see me knock out Sandy.

When Pudgy found out from Tony that Jasper had Never locked up in his meat locker, he sent some of his men over to release him. Never was so happy to be out of that cold meat locker. He may have lived in the frozen tundra of Alaska, but it felt nothing like those few hours in Jasper's meat locker waiting for him to come back and finish him off. The first thing Never asked was if one of the officers would call Rose and tell her where he was. He was wrapped up in blankets when Rose got to the Cut Above. He stood up and grabbed her in a bear hug that lifted her off her feet.

"When this is all over, would you, maybe, consider going out to dinner with me?" he said through chattering teeth. He didn't know about Sandy and Jasper. No one had told him.

"I got good news for you." Rose quickly told him what she knew from talking to the police officer who called her. Never looked very thoughtful and said, "So are you going to go to dinner with me?"

"Yes, you silly man, of course. I would think you would want to know you are a free man," she said.

"But dinner is more important," he said.

We watched as an officer was taking Sandy away in handcuffs. I felt Tony's arms tighten a little more as she passed by. I reached down and picked up the braids I pulled out and taunted her. Petty, I know, but she was going to make hamburger out of me. Tony saw what I was doing and pulled my arm down. Then, we heard a commotion at the door. I saw the officers put their hands on their guns until they heard Aunt Mae tearing Pudgy a new one until he let her and Uncle James through. They hugged me and chastised me at the same time, but I felt nothing but love. Momma and Pops had called and were both adamant that I return home at once, but that's not going to happen. I'm grown, sort of. Besides, Georgie told me last week that Momma had turned my room into a kid's room for her grandchildren when they come for a visit. My stuff was in the garage when I decided to come and retrieve it. I tried to sound a bit put out about that, but I really wasn't. It was the closure we all needed, and this was my home now.

Uncle Pete and Aunt Birdie pushed their way in. "We are family," they said to the officers at the door. They rushed over to me, and Aunt Birdie looked to see if I was in one piece.

"You scared us half to death. All those police cars, we just knew someone was dead. I was putting seed in a bird feeder and heard shots fired," said Aunt Birdie. She just kept hugging me. "I yelled at Pete, and we came running but the police wouldn't let us in."

"She waited for a while and then plowed through them like a linebacker. I followed." Uncle Pete chuckled. I noticed that Uncle James was looking at something that one of the police officers was holding. Uh-oh!

"Hey, why does my old hat and suit have all these holes in them?" said Uncle James as he took it from the officer and held it up. Since Zeke couldn't physically harm anyone, he thought he could distract Sandy until Tony got there. He put on Uncle James's suit and hat to draw her attention. He didn't know she would shoot at him. Aunt Mae saved me from having to come up with another fib.

"That old thing went out of style when Herbert Hoover was president. Should have been shot a long time ago," said Aunt Mae. We all laughed, and it felt good.

It seemed like Christmas. There was that kind of happiness and joy being spread around. It started getting late, and there was still the Celebration to go to next door. Everyone slowly said their goodbyes, and I hugged everyone as they filed out. They all headed to the Water's Edge. Tony purposely held back to be the last one. We were grinning at each other.

"I think we have some catching up to do." He turned to watch his family walk next door and smiled. "I have to get back to the bar. He moved close to give me a kiss, and my cell rang. I looked down and it was Pops.

"Hi, Pops. No, I haven't changed my mind about coming home." I looked at Tony and he smiled. He then waved and left. After I hung up, I changed into a nice outfit that even Tory would approve of. I was feeling so happy when I put on the last touches and headed next door. It felt so good to be in love with the greatest man on earth (sorry, Pops, I mean besides you). I wondered if this is how Zeke feels as he floats about. If I could sing, cartoon birds would be fluttering down and landing on my hands, little cartoon bunny rabbits would be thumping their little feet, and . . . there was a sudden movement by the boathouse. I thought I saw eyes. It took me right out of my Disney interlude. I blew out air and decided whatever it is, let it be. I've had enough excitement for this month. I headed into the Water's Edge and looked around for Tony. He was not in his usual spot behind the bar.

Still searching for Tony, I found him in a booth with a very beautiful girl. From what I could see, she had a great figure and was dressed in a pretty sundress that showed off her perfect curves and pretty bronze complexion. She wore her hair in a pageboy like Catherine Zeta-Jones did in the movie *Chicago*. It seemed old-fashioned and fashionable at the same time. She had on black high heels that I bet were Jimmy Choos. I'd give my eye teeth for those. I could see that she must have recently had a manicure. Her face was that of a model, everything perfect. Tony said something to her, and she laughed a perfect laugh. Then I saw her get up and go over to Tony's side of the booth and hug him. That was enough for me. I turned around and ran out.

I half-expected to see John sitting in his spot, but he wasn't there. I guess I was going to stay in the broken hearts' club with him after all.

"Hey, where are you going?" Great, here's lover boy now.

"I'm going home. I am really tired after all this craziness."

"But I wanted you to meet someone. Please come back."

"Tony, you are the best big brother I have. I don't want that to change. Hi, John." John came running up. "See you guys later." I turned and walked away.

"Did you tell her?" John lit up a cigarette and started to put it in his mouth. Tony, reached up behind him without taking his eyes off Billie, took it out of his hand, and stomped it out.

"No, she thinks I'm her brother."

"Her brother?"

"But I'm going to change her mind if it takes the rest of my life."

"You got it bad. She'll come to the Celebration, I'm sure. Come on, I'll buy you a drink. I know this great bartender. I got a fresh pack of cigs too." John slapped Tony on the back. They started heading back to the bar. "You know, I'm in this club for the heartbroken. You want to join? So far there are only two members. We could probably fit you in." Tony snorted and shook his head. John opened the door. You could hear the bar crowd having a good time, and then it became muffled as the door closed behind them.

When I first got back from the Water's Edge, Zeke was doing an "I told you so" dance. When I told him about Tony's girlfriend, he stopped dancing. He thought Tony was a great guy, and he is. Just not my great guy. I guess I'm going to go back to binge-watching the *Fresh Prince of Bel Air*. Zeke could tell I was depressed and disappeared. I sat there alone. Just then my ringtone played Beyonce's "No Scrubs." Great, just what I needed now for Pig Slop to call. And why is he calling me anyway? I hit Ignore. I know. I could block him, but I thought it would be more aggravating to him if I didn't. I must get my pleasure where I can get it. Especially now. I wonder if it is too late to become a nun.

I heard a car roll up and then doors slamming. In rushed my family. All of them except the girls. They were at Marcus's parents' house for the weekend. They all ran to me and hugged me and checked me all over to see if I was all in one piece. The blues that had come over me about Tony had lessened a little. Eventually Pops said, "Well, are we going over? I don't want to miss it."

"What are you talking about, Pops? And how did you all get here so fast?"

"The Celebration. We were in the car on our way up when this all happened. Come on, let's go."

"And now we have even more to celebrate. So, let's go. I want to see Birdie and Pete. I haven't seen them in a while," Momma said.

"I think I'm going to pass. It has been some evening, and I'm a little bit tired." I tried to worm my way out. I just couldn't stand to see Tony and his girlfriend together.

"Auh, come on. We haven't had a night out in while. We seldom have time away from the girls. I want to dance with the she-ro at least once if my wife will let me." He smiled.

"Just once but the rest of the dances are mine." Georgie smiled. "If he steps on your feet, Billie, don't be surprised." Everyone got up and started heading for the backdoor. I didn't want to dampen their fun, so I got up and joined them. We walked through the backdoor of the Water's Edge. We knew most of the people there, and they all cheered when I came in. News travels fast in the Village. They all knew about what happened with Jasper and Sandy and my part in it. I don't know how they all knew so quickly—oh, that darn Georgie. I looked over at her, and she shrugged and smiled. She was clearly proud of me.

CHAPTER 36

It was like a reunion for my family. They missed all their summer friends. While they talked and asked questions about what happened, I glanced over at the booth where Tony and his girlfriend had been sitting. There was a young distinguished-looking black man whom I didn't know sitting there in an army uniform. Then I noticed that most of the tables and chairs had been moved so that there was a large open space in the middle of the bar.

John walked up to us and told us to follow him. We did, to a couple of tables where his parents were already sitting next to Aunt Mae and Uncle James. After everyone hugged and got caught up on the recent events, we all sat down. John came over to me and said to me, "Just sit here and things will come into focus."

Then he signaled someone, and the lights momentarily went out, and we were draped in darkness. When the lights came back on there was a man dressed in black form-fitting pants and a white shirt that was partially open in the front, posed in the middle of the floor. Everyone started clapping. The man's head was bowed, and his face was partially hidden by the black fedora he was wearing. Even so, I knew instantly that it was Tony. When the clapping quieted down, music started to play. I recognized the music. It was the tango music from the movie *True Lies*. Me and Georgie must have seen that movie a hundred times.

Then, out of the shadows, Tony's girlfriend came slowly sauntering in. She was breathtaking in a beautiful red gown with a slit on the side all the way up to Canada. When she walked, she showed a long shapely leg. I bet it took her half the day to shave it. Her back was bare, and she had on very high heels. She was so perfect that I could see what Tony saw in her. Geesh! I'd date her. I'm just saying. I felt sick.

Tony threw his hat into the audience, and they began to dance a tango that was the most beautiful thing I ever saw. My jaw dropped open. I was in awe. It was sensuous and sexy. They had such perfect timing it was as if they were one person. I was really feeling low. When the dance was over, the bar went wild. We got up from our seats, and everyone but me crowded around them. The man in the uniform had reached Tony's girlfriend, and they were hugging and kissing like crazy. Wait, what? What the heck was going on?

Tony looked in the crowd until he found me, and he fish-tailed his way over to me.

"I'm glad you changed your mind and came," he said. He was a bit out of breath.

"You were wonderful. You both were. Wow!" I was still trying to process what I saw.

"I want you to meet her," he said dragging me behind him over to where she was now sitting in the soldier's lap. Hey, now I am really confused. "Honey and David, I want you to meet Billie. Billie, David was my best buddy in college. He's been over in Iraq for six months. This is his wife, Honey." Her name is *Honey*. Oh boy. Now things were coming into focus as John predicted. And where is John? I bet he knew all along, that slug.

"Tony was my best man at our wedding and my stand-in for Honey's dance contest. I owe you a lot, man," David said as they gripped each other's hands in a handshake. His eyes turned to his beautiful wife. She looked at him with such love. "I don't think I could have pulled that dance off as well as you did, man."

"No worries. It was fun. And we came in second in the contest so that was great, huh, Honey?"

"Yes. I thought I was going to have to drop out since my sweety deployed unexpectanly. All the time David was gone, all I did was worry about him." She was looking at her husband as she spoke. "I guess that was when he called Tony and asked him to stand in for him to get my mind on something else. All the rehearsing and planning for it helped keep me sane." She turned to me and said, "I'm so glad we finally got to meet. Tony talks about you all the time." He does? Boy, I may have been able to solve a murder, but I suck at figuring out my own love life.

Tony was looking at me like he had made up his mind about something.

170

"Excuse us a minute. I need to talk to Billie alone," he said, dragging me behind him. We went outside in the moonlight. There were stars everywhere, but to be real, it could be raining. It didn't matter. I was feeling good. He didn't have a secret girlfriend.

"Why didn't you tell me about Honey?" I said indignantly. "You could have just said it instead of being so mysterious. And having John and probably Tory in on it too. Why I shouldn't be speaking to you at all. And who got you the Sexy shirt?" I don't know why I can't just let things go. As Wilma Flintstone once said, "She who plays hard to get, doesn't get got."

"Even now you want to fight with me?" he said. There was enough moonlight that I could see he was smiling. I was smiling too. That cheesy smile that isn't easily removable. "I wanted to make sure you wanted to stay without any influence. You had so much going on I didn't want to add to the pressure. But when I heard those gunshots, I thought . . ." He didn't say it. "So, are you going to keep arguing with me or what?"

"Well, probably. I told you I was messy. You know me." He nodded.

"Yes, and for some crazy reason, I have loved you all my life." He was still holding my hand.

"You have?" And there it was. *Thee*, not the, *thee* best feeling in the world. I took a deep breath. My heart was racing.

"I have. Oh, and I'm over being your brother." I saw Zeke in one of the windows at the Inn looking at us. I couldn't tell for sure from this distance, but I'm sure his eyebrows were going up and down.

"Well, what do you plan to do about it? I may have other options I need to look into." I saw what I wanted to see in the challenge I threw down.

"Well, I . . ." I didn't give him a chance to finish. I pulled him to me and kissed him. He embraced me and responded to my kiss.

Inside the Water's Edge, most of the people were peeking outside watching Billie and Tony. Their hands were cupped over their eyes to the window so that they could see. When they saw them kissing, they all cheered.

"It's about time. I thought they would never figure it out," said Uncle Pete, and everyone laughed. "Now this is a celebration. I'm buying." Everyone cheered again. "John, give me one drink and thirty straws." Everyone started laughing again.

EPILOGUE

One evening I coaxed Zeke outside. Zeke said he hadn't been outside in over a hundred years. We were sitting down by the lake. Well, I was sitting. I guess you could say Zeke was sitting too, but it was on top of an unopened umbrella. I guess sitting on the point of an umbrella doesn't hurt the passed over like it would the living.

The weather had changed, and spring was starting to feel like summer. I was looking forward to the Inn having its first guest arriving in a couple of days, but even so, it was nice to have this peace after all we had recently been through. Zeke and I made a weird companionship, like Martha Stewart and Snoop Dogg. It worked for them, and it seemed to work for us.

"Ah, Billie?" Zeke broke the silence.

"Yes, Zeke?" I took a sip of my lemonade.

"I'm so glad you found love. You needed it. But I was also thinking . . ."

"Go ahead and say it. What are you thinking? That maybe I should tell Tony about you? I thought about that too, and I don't know how to even begin." I didn't know how I should approach that or how he would take it.

"No, actually, I was thinking we should get a dog."

"A dog? We have an Inn. How would we take care of a dog?" Don't get me wrong. I would love to have a dog. But thoughts of me being the one taking care of it seemed to outweigh the benefit for an innkeeper. Plus I doubt Zeke would be much help. There's only so much a ghost can do. "We would have to go through potty training, and the dog would have to be walked, get shots. And what if we had guests who didn't care for pets or had an allergy?" Before I could go on with my thoughts on the subject, Zeke interrupted them.

"No. No we wouldn't. I kinda already have one." Before I could say anything, Zeke put his fingers in his teeth and whistled. From behind the boathouse came the cutest partially invisible cocker spaniel ghost dog you ever didn't see. Geesh! I'm going to need something stronger than lemonade.